THE PLAGUE

THE PLAGUE

Feather and Bone

The Crow Chronicles

Clem Martini

KCP FICTION
An Imprint of Kids Can Press

KCP Fiction is an imprint of Kids Can Press

Kids Can Press acknowledges the financial support of the Government of Ontario, through the Ontario Media Development Corporation's Ontario Book Initiative; the Ontario Arts Council; the Canada Council for the Arts; and the Government of Canada, through the BPIDP, for our publishing activity.

Published in Canada by
Kids Can Press Ltd.
29 Birch Avenue
Toronto, ON M4V 1E2

Published in the U.S. by
Kids Can Press Ltd.
2250 Military Road
Tonawanda, NY 14150

www.kidscanpress.com

Edited by Charis Wahl
Designed by Marie Bartholomew
Printed and bound in Canada
This book is printed on acid-free paper that is 100% ancient forest friendly (100% post-consumer recycled).

CM 05 0 9 8 7 6 5 4 3 2 1

Library and Archives Canada Cataloguing in Publication

Martini, Clem, 1956–
The plague / Clem Martini.

(Feather and bone)

ISBN 1-55337-666-8 (bound). ISBN 1-55337-667-6 (pbk.)

I. Title. II. Series: Martini, Clem, 1956– . Feather and bone.

PS8576.A7938P53 2005 jC813'.54 C2004-906036-8

Kids Can Press is a Corus™ Entertainment company

Crows are the strong survivors they are partially because they are such a fiercely loyal, adaptable and resilient bunch. My own, much treasured family also possesses these traits in abundance. Cheryl, Chandra and Miranda — many, many thanks for your support. All my love to you, and as always, Good Eating!

ACKNOWLEDGMENTS

Many thanks are owed to a flock of folks who have helped me out and shown me kindnesses along the way to producing this book. All the dauntless Martinis, Foggos and Lamoureuxs. The people at Kids Can who worked so diligently to make this book and this series everything it could be — and above all Charis Wahl, my genial editor and fellow crow enthusiast. Janine Cheeseman for her continuing encouragement. All the thoughtful people who read the rough drafts and offered their helpful comments: the Mother/Daughter Book Club crew, the Baxters, Lunns, Poriskys, Strongs and Towers; Janet Lee-Evoy; Katie, Jason, Betty and John Poulsen; Emily, Anna, and Brian Cooley, and Mary Ann Wilson. Vanessa Valdes and George Babiak, who were especially gracious hosts when I was perched in their home performing avian research. And Cheri Macaulay for her inspirational crow vision.

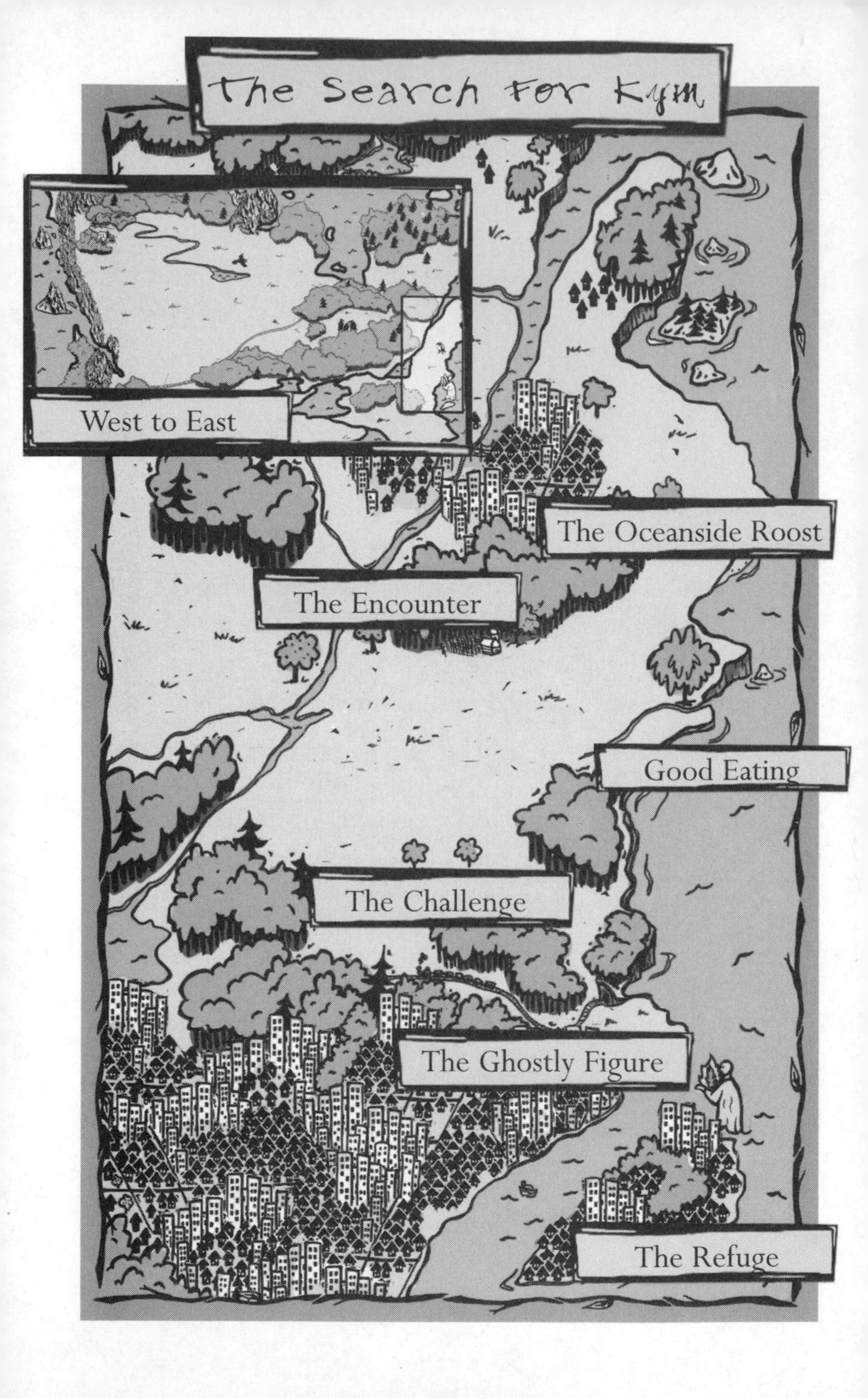
The Search for Kym
West to East
The Oceanside Roost
The Encounter
Good Eating
The Challenge
The Ghostly Figure
The Refuge

Part One

Chapter 1

Draw in, find your place on the branch and know this: Dreams are sacred.

When we sleep, we see life as the Maker first saw us. We are, after all, what the Maker dreamed in her long night alone. The stories revealed to us when we dream, then, aren't just images shaped by night and mist, but things we must grasp and remember. Once we wake, who knows what action we will be directed to take?

Cousins, listen! Some of the things I will tell you I have lived.

Some of the things I will tell you I have dreamed.

Some of the things I will tell you may have dreamed me.

And that may make them all the truer.

Dream with me now, and see how I have seen things, dreamed things, and come to this place. Watch with me as three Crows approach across a stretch of rolling hills. It is late spring. The sun glitters low in the west, and from a distance they are not immediately distinguishable one from the other, three black crescents flickering in the glare. One flies with the slow, energy-saving strokes of the elderly. A younger one flies with thoughtful and direct strokes immediately beside the elder, her head cocked in his direction, as though listening to something being said. And the third flies with urgency and impatience, rushing above, over and ahead of the other two, then slowing for them to catch up.

These three approach low over tall grasses that ripple and shimmer like waves before wind on the surface of the ocean. The shadow of each bird stretches and races ahead, long and lean. Listen. As they fly, their voices lift and rise across the field and across time as well, because these events have occurred in the past.

"No," the restless one argued and swept back to join the others as he made his point. "No, it's not —"

"That's not what I'm saying, Kyp —"

"Kym, are you saying —" he interrupted her, only to be interrupted in turn.

"How can you possibly tell what I'm *saying* when you aren't even *listening* to me?"

"I *am* listening. I am listening and, are you saying — are you saying, because it sounds like this is what you are saying — are you saying that *no* ceremony can be changed —"

"Don't be an idiot," Kym snorted. "Of course that's not what I'm *saying*." The way she said "idiot" was fond. These were friends disagreeing.

"Well, have you been listening to me?"

"Have either of you," the older one interrupted patiently, "been listening to the other?"

"Because," Kyp continued, "because if we can't *change* anything, then we can't *fix* anything either, and *something* has to change. Three good Crows were Banished just this winter. And for *what*?"

"I know, and I'm not saying that things can't change."

"Good. Because they've got to, Kym. They've *got* to change."

"And they will, Kyp. And we'll make those changes. But not all at once. We can't just push these older ones out —"

"Calm yourselves," Kalum interrupted again. "Some things will change and some won't, and you will be surprised to discover how much and how little you have to do with either. You will both have to deal with more pressing situations than this —

and lead in a calmer and more reasonable fashion than either of you have demonstrated here."

"I'm sorry, Kalum," Kym apologized immediately.

"And I'm sorry," Kyp echoed. "It's just that there are so many things to be done."

"Well. Let's move on to something else," said Kalum. "Tomorrow there is a Naming. Which of you can be expected to lead the Family in the Recollection of Names?"

"I could do that," Kym offered, after exchanging glances with Kyp, "if you'd like, Uncle."

"Very well," Kalum said and nodded. "And what is the first thing that must be done after the Family is assembled for the ceremony?"

"I will lead the Family in prayer."

"And then?"

"And then we will recite the Long Flight, Chooser to Chooser from the First Nest on."

"Very good," Kalum murmured. "And you can recite it, of course, Kyp?" A silence followed. "That would be *you* I was asking, Kyp."

"I *think* so," Kyp answered hesitantly.

"Think?" Kalum repeated.

"I just have some trouble with the middle portion —"

"*Middle* portion?" Kalum sighed. "There is no *middle* portion. That's your trouble. You think of it as a list, but for it to live in you it has to become *more* than a list. More than a series of events."

Kyp returned a glance that said he understood nothing of what had been said.

"But it *is* a list," he maintained. "A long list."

Kalum squinted at Kyp and then began patiently. "Your name is you? That's correct? That is, it describes you. Yes?"

Kyp nodded.

"So, tell me, which of your names is you? Are you *Kyp*, or are you *Kurea*, or are you *Kinaar*?"

"All of those things."

"*Exactly. All* of those things. All of those things is not a list. It is *you*. You. You are not Kyp *or* Kurea *or* Kinaar — you are Kyp of the Kurea Clan of the Family Kinaar. One Crow. What you deliver to the Family isn't a list, it is a Chant of Remembrance, and *everything* in it is connected from beginning to end. Do you see?"

"I think so," Kyp said hesitantly.

"Well, I'm not sure that you do. But perhaps by repeating it one more time you will begin to understand it more fully. Let's go over it as we fly."

Kyp stifled a sigh and began. "From the nest of Great Crow came the First Brood —"

Kalum nodded his approval, glanced up and over a shoulder, then abruptly turned and broke left.

"Fly!" he shouted.

The Crows scattered over the prairie grass. From above, a thunderbolt of feathers and talons struck, snapping a clump of grass and dirt through the air. Out of the cloud of debris and dust, a scream of frustration sounded, and an adult golden eagle emerged, wheeled, recovered and without hesitation selected the oldest and slowest of the Crows.

chapter 2

There is almost nothing to an eagle that isn't talon, wing, muscle or beak, so there's no point trying to outfly them — they're that much stronger, larger and better equipped than we are. A single outstretched wing of a mature eagle can eclipse an entire Crow. But if an eagle can't be outflown, it can be evaded.

The three Crows plunged down a gully and dropped into a tangle of scrub poplar and willow, cutting and swerving between stalk and stem. The older Crow pulled ahead and slid between an upraised fork. The eagle grasped air, effortlessly flipped sideways and slipped through, closing the gap. As it did so, Kym folded her wings and dropped from above, knocking the eagle on its right shoulder. The eagle narrowly avoided a tree limb, screamed and launched itself at its attacker. Kym dodged a slash of its hooked beak and cut through a twisted knot of vine and debris dangling from a poplar. When she appeared on the other side, the eagle had already arrived.

Kyp swooped under a branch and emerged beneath the eagle, tugging at its left flank and throwing it off balance. It recovered and quickly struck at Kyp with a talon. Kyp looped overtop the slash, rolled over the wing and rapped the side of the eagle's head. A willow suddenly loomed, separating Kyp from the struggle. Kym slid in and plucked a beak full of feathers from the eagle's left shoulder. The eagle spun much more quickly than Kym had expected, and all at once she found herself wedged between the trunk of a poplar and the eagle's outstretched wings, with no room to escape. Kyp crashed through the branches above onto the eagle's broad back and settled on the right wing, plunging his talons into its upper shoulder. The eagle screamed, jerked its head around and caught Kyp, throwing him sprawling against the tree trunk. Then, free of all three Crows for the moment, the eagle banked right through an opening between willows and, with a final glance backward, disappeared.

Kyp, Kym and Kalum spun and wove through the trees until they were certain they were no longer being chased, then dropped to a perch, panting and gulping air.

"Well, that," Kalum said between gasps, "was careless of us. Anyone hurt?"

Kym spied scattered red drops gathering on a branch. "Kyp, you're bleeding."

"It caught me with the tip of its beak on the edge of my left wing."

"Let's see," Kalum said and moved closer to inspect the cut. After a moment, he relaxed. "It's not deep. It should stop shortly." He glanced up at Kyp. "But, Kyp, that wasn't necessary. That eagle wasn't even gracing us with its full concentration. We could have led it in and around the trees in a game of tag until it was so dizzy and tired it would have been happy to return to its roost for a little nap."

"But —"

"Listen to me," Kalum continued patiently. "No one will ever question your bravery — we all know you're brave. You proved yourself many times over when you battled the cats in the tunnel last year. But you have to learn to avoid a fight at all costs. You are only as strong as a single feather. One snapped plume in your forewing, or a couple of feathers plucked from your tail, and you are no longer able to fly — and if you can't fly, you can't fight, lead or escape. Fight only when you absolutely must, and above all do not let your opponent choose the battle. Never fight an eagle like an eagle. Unless you fly — and fight — like a Crow, you will always, always be at a disadvantage."

Kyp nodded. "I understand."

"I'm not sure you do. But perhaps in time you will." Then the old bird spread his wings and flinched. "Look at that," he clucked, shaking his head. "A sure sign of my sad decline. I didn't engage in any of the wrangling, yet I've managed to pull a muscle in my left wing." He glanced about at the grove of alders they had come to rest among. The trees formed a tiny, tangled solitude. "I'll roost here tonight."

Kym shot him a glance. "Alone?"

"No, niece. I spied your disapproval. Kyp, you'll stay with me and help an old fellow out. We two poor invalids will keep each other company. Kym, fly back to the Gathering Tree and let the Family know I'll return tomorrow by first sixth, in time for the Naming."

Kym leaned in next to the older Crow and then flew off. Kyp followed Kym a little way. They stopped at the edge of the open prairie to perform one last survey.

"Thanks," Kym said in low voice. "I know you threw yourself at the eagle because you thought *I* was in trouble."

Kyp shook his head. "He was right. I was careless."

"Listen to me. I'm telling you something. *You* were right, too. You were right for reasons Kalum couldn't see. And I'm trying to thank you for it. Now, are you okay? Is that cut bad?"

"No. It's just a little sore. It's already stopped bleeding."

"Well, keep your eyes open. You smell of blood, and who knows what that might draw out here tonight. Roost higher in the tree. You'll catch more wind, but —"

"We will."

"And keep a watch above. Uncle was right — that eagle was just testing us. It might try something more serious later if it thinks you're not alert."

"Don't worry," Kyp assured her. "And we'll join you by second sixth at the latest."

"All right. I'm going." She raised her wings and grimaced. "Eww. I feel exhausted after that chase."

Briefly they rested their heads against each other. Kym murmured "Good eating," then dropped from the branch and slipped through the brush and out over the field. Kyp watched a moment, then returned to the poplar grove.

Kalum remained resting on the branch where Kyp had left him, fastidiously rearranging the feathers of his left wing and watching Kym as she doubled back to ensure she wasn't being followed.

He cocked an eye at Kyp. "Smart girl. She will make a very good Chooser." He tugged a feather up and gently folded it back into place. "As will you."

They sat and listened to the sounds rise from the valley. Ducks and geese squawked among the reeds. Below the grove of trees, the river chuckled quietly. Above it, the wind sighed and muttered, whispering softly of its long, restless journey.

"Uncle?" Kyp said at last.

"Yes, Nephew?"

"I would rather the Choice passed to someone else."

Kalum nodded. "You've made that abundantly clear. Now, may I suggest that you get over it?"

"You don't understand," Kyp said, shaking his head. "Kym has exactly the right temperament to be Chooser. She's smart. She thinks before she speaks, she knows how to listen. I'm not good at *any* of those things. I anger too quickly. I hold grudges. I speak without thinking. Last year I managed to organize our Family in the tunnel to fight the cats because … Because someone *had* to. And I was the only one who knew where the tunnels were. So it came down to me to lead the

Family there to find shelter during the storm. And it was fine fighting the Red, because it was at least partially my responsibility that we were there at all. Besides, fighting isn't a problem for me. But the decisions that go with leading a flock — the planning, the consulting, the knowing what to do. I don't have any of that. I don't know if I ever will. I'm just — not ready."

"You are," Kalum insisted.

"I don't even know the stories," Kyp protested.

"You know them."

Kyp shook his head again. "Not the way *you* do."

"And I'm not leaving, Nephew. And you'll keep learning them. And Kym knows the ones you don't. That is why you've both been selected to Choose. You'll be a different kind of Chooser. Don't you see, you and Kym are held in very high regard because of the roles you played in saving the Family last year from the storm and the cats. The Kinaar will at least accept the *possibility* of change if it comes from *you*. And you're absolutely right — we need to change.

"I couldn't lead the Family that way," Kalum continued. "I'm too much of a curmudgeon and set in my habits. But you and Kym, you just might be able to." Kalum rubbed his neck against a branch, stretched and settled in the crook between branch and trunk. "You're young, and you think that

Choosers have always been like me. They haven't. Different individuals are chosen for different times. Believe me, my time has passed."

Kyp selected a broad branch to the right of Kalum and folded his legs beneath him. "With all due respect, the Family will find that both Kym and I fall short of your abilities."

"Don't make me out to be more than I am," the older bird warned. "I was a very imperfect Chooser."

"You won't find anyone in the Family who says that."

Kalum shook a mosquito off his forehead. "Oh, maybe not today. But it *has* been said, believe me — and worse. And the Crows who said it haven't always been wrong." He chuckled ruefully. "To be a Chooser you have to love the Family — but you have to love carefully. Me, I've always loved the talk of Crows a little too much. The sound of Crows in a tree late at night, the sound of one Crow calling to another as we fly through the twilight during migration. And the sound of my own voice — my biggest weakness. I've always loved talk a little too much. When everyone else has shut up, I still have a beakful of things to say. The Family could use Choosers who don't enjoy words as much as I do. Frankly, I feel quite certain that the Family will be relieved to have Choosers who talk less than I do."

"You're wrong," Kyp objected. "They'll miss you and want you back the moment you fold your wings."

"Nonsense! In the two of you, the Family will be provided with choice as it never has before. If nothing else, you two will confuse everyone so badly they won't know how to deal with you. Now, shh," Kalum said, and grimaced. "I need rest."

Kyp glanced at the older bird with concern. "Are you all right?"

"I'm fine. It's just been a long Gathering. A long Gathering, a long day and a long life. It's chilly and my bones ache."

They sat silently in the tree. The mist gathered and settled on the river. The fading sun's delicate rays pierced the narrow gaps in the trees and lit the haze like a fine golden spider's web settling over the valley.

"Look at us perched here — and all of *that* sits out there," Kalum said, nodding at the valley below. "We talk and talk about ourselves, but that's just vanity. We are only ever perched on the edge of something much larger than ourselves."

At last the sun eased behind the mountains and, after a brief display of glory, slipped away into a thick, rich darkness. The silence grew, and the two Crows fell asleep.

Chapter 3

"Kyp. Kyp!"

The voice summoned him from a great distance. Kyp's head throbbed, and a fire seemed to burn just beneath his feathers. He closed his eyes tighter and tried to still the pain.

"Kyp!" the voice called again, louder.

He opened his eyes. Light flooded in, hot and bright. Quickly, he shut them again. What was happening? Where was he?

"Kyp. Wake up!" the voice sounded again, more insistent. Where had he heard that voice before? He forced one eye open and squinted through the glare. It was Kort, a thin, retiring Crow from the Kemna Clan.

"What is it?" Kyp croaked, his throat dry.

"Kyp, it took me forever to find you. You've got to come right away. There's … It's … I can't …" Kyp couldn't see the Crow except as a blurry silhouette framed against the bright light, but his voice was overcome by emotion. "… describe what's happened."

Kyp tried to make sense of what he was being told. "Come where?" he finally rasped, his tongue unusually thick in his beak. "What's happened?"

"Terrible things!" Kort blurted. "A sickness … some kind of, disease … struck the Family. I don't know when exactly. During the night, or late afternoon, a day and a half ago. It hit Keru first. He dropped from the branch, just after moonrise. Like a stone. Since then, it's been … Nearly fifty Crows have died. Others are still sick and may die yet …"

A day and a half ago? What was he talking about? Kyp forced himself to open both eyes.

"Kort," he interrupted, "what about Kym?"

"She's sick, too, but, Kyp —"

"What? How sick?"

"I don't know, but …"

Kyp found it hard to focus, and Kort's inability to finish sentences made it doubly difficult. "*But what?*" he snapped, instantly regretting his outburst.

"The humans."

"The humans? What humans? What are you talking about?"

Kort made an effort to slow down. "A number of Crows collapsed early in the day. Kym was one of them. Nobody knew what was happening. We thought she was dead — several of those that fell had died. But she — about mid-sixth the next day — she raised her head and crawled to the base of the tree. Lay there, panting. Then humans arrived. Two of them — in white skins that covered everything, even their heads and paws — and they gathered up all the Crows that were sick but still alive. They took Kym, Kwakalum, Klykwyt —"

"Wait!" Kyp tried to catch his breath as his heart raced. "Kym? Where? Where did they take her?"

Kort shrugged. "The Great Crow only knows. They carried her and the others into one of their moving boxes, and then … She could be anywhere."

"Didn't anyone follow the moving box?"

The small bird shook his head. "How could we? Hardly anyone was around anymore. Anyone healthy, anyway. The Family has scattered. I'm one of the last here and I'm only here because —"

Kyp opened his wings. Why did they feel so heavy? "I have to go look for her."

"Wait! There's more."

Kyp halted.

"I'm trying to tell you something else. I came looking to tell you. I found Kalum —"

Kyp's heart sank. "He's caught the sickness, too?"

"What? Maybe. I'm not sure." Kort faltered. "But, it's worse than that."

"How?" It was hard to imagine anything worse.

"Oh, Kyp." His voice cracked. "It looks like he's been attacked. He's not moving. When I saw him, he could barely speak. He told me to find you —"

"Take me to him."

"Follow me," Kort said, then added nervously, "but don't come too close as we fly."

Chapter 4

The mid-sixth. Sun directly overhead and its rays had never felt so hot. Kyp's wings hung heavy, each stroke an effort. As the two Crows flew, Kyp tried to organize his thoughts, but like his body, his mind refused to work properly.

"It looks to me," Kort said, "like you have it, too. Maybe the early stages. If it doesn't get worse than this, you might make it."

"Thanks," Kyp muttered, but Kort didn't appear to hear him.

To the right, on the ground, Kyp's eye caught sight of the still body of a Crow lying atop a bush. Moments later, he spotted a dog trotting by, something black and limp dangling from its mouth.

Kort caught Kyp's expression and nodded. "It's not just here. You'll find remains everywhere. I'm afraid to look too closely. Afraid I'll catch it, too."

Kyp's heart dropped as he began to realize the extent of the disaster. Kort suddenly dipped a wing. "If you want to find Kalum, he's there. Near the bend in the river."

Kyp made out a wing and a leg, half sheltered beneath a sprawling gooseberry bush. He dropped to the ground. As he approached, the old Crow opened one eye.

"Nephew. Good eating," he rasped, his voice dry and distant.

Kyp sank to his haunches beside Kalum. "Good eating, Uncle. What's happened?"

"I woke sick and terribly thirsty. It was still early. I flew here to get a drink. Didn't keep my top eye open. Was hit."

"The eagle?"

"No, no." He quickly drew a breath and released a ragged sigh. "No. It was the last thing I expected." He sighed again. "The last thing."

Kyp waited, but Kalum lay quietly, eyes closed, breathing. When it appeared that he wasn't going to speak, Kyp prompted him again. "What?"

"Family," Kalum said without opening his eyes.

"What do you mean?" Kyp asked, but Kalum didn't respond. "Kalum?"

Slowly Kalum seemed to pull himself back from a distant place. He scanned the surroundings carefully. "This is a beautiful place, don't you think?" Kyp looked about at the mud, the twigs and scum spinning in an eddy along the edge of the bank. Kalum drew a long breath. "This land in the shadow of the mountains. I have never enjoyed it so much as this year."

"Kalum," Kyp persisted, "what did you mean when you said 'Family'?"

Kalum shifted his position and groaned. "I was hit. From above."

"Yes, I know. By *what* though?"

Suddenly Kalum glanced about. "Where's Kym?"

"Humans have her."

"Humans have her?" Kalum coughed and struggled to lift his head. "How's that possible?"

"I don't know. I've just heard. She and some others got sick. Humans captured a number of the Family. Kort just —"

He looked about and realized that Kort, having fulfilled his obligations, had fled.

Kalum peered intently at Kyp. "You have to find her."

"How?"

"Look for her!" Kalum said between coughs.

"I will," Kyp replied, trying to ease the older Crow.

Kalum drew another rattling breath, held it and

slowly exhaled. When he opened his eyes, they weren't focused.

"Yes. I kept a poor watch. A very poor watch. That's always been my problem."

"What?" Kyp asked.

"Should have watched more and talked less. I've always talked too much."

His beak closed, and that was the last breath Kalum took.

Chapter 5

The dark, familiar body of Kalum seemed suddenly small and frail, splayed on the mud, his wings askew, head resting on a patch of leaves. Kyp closed his eyes and waited for the spasm of grief to pass. In that one moment, everything collapsed in on him: the sickness and the loss of the Family. The disappearance of Kym. And now Kalum, a Crow he had known all his life, a Crow he had respected, and who had looked after him. When he opened his eyes again, he realized how alone he was. Kyp gazed down at his elder's body and gently prodded it with the tip of his beak.

"Kalum?" he urged gently.

"Just scavenge now."

For a brief moment, Kyp thought he had only imagined the voice. Then he heard a low laugh.

High above him — so high no features could be made out — was the silhouette of a Crow, circling slowly.

"Gone to the Maker," the voice called down.

Kyp rose on unsteady legs. "Who are you?" he shouted, the sound of his voice hurting his head.

The laughter drifting down was his only reply.

He squinted against the glare. "Who are you?"

High up over the river, the figure was winging his way across the valley. "Someone," the Crow called over his shoulder, "who knows what happened to your Chooser."

Chapter 6

Kyp followed the Crow, his chest aching. Though he flew as fast as he was able, the distance between the two never lessened.

The chase took them well into the latter sixth. A wind sprang up from the west, and clouds gathered. Kyp followed, burning from the inside as fever slowly scorched his body.

The incline of the countryside grew steeper. Hills folded, warped and grew. A mountain rose at the junction of two long, winding valleys. The winds funneled through the passes, sweeping clouds ahead of them. Great roiling thunderheads gathered and stacked one on the other. The Crow disappeared into a cloud near the mountain crest, and Kyp feared he had lost him — until he heard laughter.

Chapter 7

As Kyp flew higher, the storm opened up. What sort of bad things are there in a storm? On a day like this, you find out. Lightning. Thunder. Bursts of sleet. Tiny, stinging pellets of hail. Rain, slashing like talons and beaks. Kyp fought on through the murk. Then a blinding flash of light sparked and the sky split.

It is said that lightning is the fiery tongue of the World Snake. When that monstrous serpent writhes out of its lair under mountains and coils about in the sky, its tongue darts out — lightning crisscrosses the sky — and anything it touches is drawn into the great snake's mouth and disappears forever.

Kyp felt his feathers rise as the smell of lightning lingered.

At the mountain's very summit, a tiny gray dot of a lake emerged, deep and clear, set in a towering ring of crumbling cliffs. Stunted fir trees and creeping juniper fringed the lake, the occasional scorched tree limb attesting to past storms.

Kyp shook the rain from his eyes and scanned the clouds as they boiled over the summit. Finding nothing, he flew low over the dwarf trees, searching each one carefully.

Abruptly, blinding light shredded the sky again. An explosion of hot air buffeted Kyp, flinging him backward, just as a figure hurtled toward him, talons tearing into his right wing, lifting then tossing him. Kyp fell, grabbed air and fell some more.

A voice echoed off the cliffs. "In the old tongue, this place is called Lightning Lives Here. I call it the Proving Ground. The Maker plays tag with you here. Can you survive the game? Are you strong enough?"

Kyp scoured the clouds. Nothing. "You said you knew what happened to our Chooser," he called.

"You're sturdier than he was," the voice called from a different direction. Kyp scanned the rocky cliffs. "I struck him only once — and he never climbed back to his talons."

Kyp felt rage burn through him. As if it would have taken skill to knock down someone as old and sick as Kalum.

"Are you afraid?" Kyp shouted. "Afraid to let me know who you are?"

No answer emerged from the clouds.

Kyp understood this about any air battle: whoever owns the height wins. He caught an updraft, tucked a wing into it and spiraled up. Winds bounced off the cliff walls, buffeting him from all angles. He glanced down. The big Crow was climbing after him, curling and curling, slipping through a cloud, disappearing, then reappearing. Kyp made a quick decision. As the stranger emerged from one cloud, Kyp plummeted, catching him on the tip of his wing just as the air was again ripped apart by lightning. The force of the explosion thrust the air from Kyp's lungs. When he recovered consciousness, he was falling and the stranger was on him again, clawing. He sensed the weight of the attack bearing him down — then heard a pop, felt a tearing in his shoulder and a searing bolt of pain run through his entire right side.

The attack had lasted only an instant. The Crow had slipped away once more into the shadows and clouds. With one wing broken, Kyp knew he couldn't possibly survive another attack. His only hope was to keep out of the stranger's way and use the mountain's cover. He dropped to ground level and sped through stunted trees, under branches and over. Keep moving, he thought. Keep changing course. Abruptly, branches burst to his right, needles and twigs scattered. Pain shot up his right wing and he fell.

A voice woke him. "'Just ask her.' The last thing I said to you. I gave you my food offering and asked you to give it to her and see if she would make a match. Tell me, did you? Or did you forget about me?"

Kyp was sprawled on a coarse, scratchy patch of juniper. He tried to lift his right wing and felt it throb.

"Kuper?"

"Now" — the underbrush parted, and a tall form stepped between two branches — "you begin to remember."

"Kuper," Kyp repeated. "How? I thought you were dead. I thought the cats had killed you. Your body was gone. I went back to check."

Kuper was even taller than Kyp remembered him and was even more imposing as his feathers rose around his nape and crown. "Yes, gone," Kuper murmured and stepped forward. "But not missed, maybe? Maybe you said to yourself a dog picked him up and carried him away. Why not? That happens."

"What did happen?" Kyp asked.

"Many things. Many things," Kuper rumbled and moved closer to Kyp. "I lay in the snow a long time. My heart stopped. I went to another world. The Maker flies there, and there are perches prepared for guests. But the Maker had something else in mind for me. When I woke, I didn't find myself dangling from the teeth of a dog. Instead I found my wings bound. Unable to fly. Pawed. Clutched close to a human."

Kuper stopped moving, captured by the memory.

"I *wanted* to die," he continued, almost to himself. "If dying was something you could will, I would be dead. The human carried me back to its roost — and all the other humans. Shoved me in a woven enclosure of stone. No way out. No fresh air. No room to fly. Just enough space to survive, day after day. I refused to eat and hoped I would starve. The human pried my beak open. Forced food down.

"Finally, one night, alone in the dark, confined, I decided the Maker had kept me alive for a reason. I stopped fighting. I pretended to be tamed. Pretended to accept the humans' food, their help, their touch. I trained myself to stay calm and still when they loomed, their immense faces crushing up next to mine, their reeking breath surrounding me. I waited.

"One day my waiting paid off. When the human came to feed me it left the entrance to the stone nest open. I bit its paw, clawed its limbs and threw myself out of the opening, out of the enclosure and out of the human roost. I flew as hard as I could. Flew long after the human and its roost had disappeared. Flew until the rushing air had scoured me of all the clinging, stinking, sticking human smell. It was then I knew why the Maker had kept me alive. For one reason — revenge. Upon humans. Upon those who gave me up. Who left me helpless for the humans to find." Slowly, Kuper's head revolved until he looked directly at Kyp. "And above all, on you."

Kyp's wing ached, and the fever made thinking difficult, but he raised his head and looked straight at Kuper. "I thought you were dead," he said simply. "I never would have left you otherwise."

For a long time Kuper said nothing. "Dead. That would have been good, wouldn't it? Convenient? And we'll never know how things might have gone between Kym and me, because now *she's* dead —"

A knot tightened in Kyp's stomach. "What do you mean?"

"I flew past the Gathering Tree searching and felt sick as I began to understand what had happened. Realized just how late I had left things when I saw Kym's dead body on the ground along with all the others. But if I was too late for some things, there was still time to do others. I went looking for you. Instead I found Kalum."

"You arrived too *early*," Kyp said bitterly.

"What are you talking about?"

"Kym's not dead. If you thought she was, it was because you arrived while she was still unconscious. She fell from her perch and lay still for some time — which must have been when you saw her — but she was still alive when she was carried away by the human."

Kuper's feathers stuck straight out. "You're making this up."

"Kort saw it. Saw them take her away."

Kuper was struck dumb by the information. Kyp stood. "You killed Kalum — a Crow who had only fondness for you — because he left you for the human, and now the human has Kym and it's *your* fault. You might have prevented it. You might have done something to help Kym. The human has her and it's because of *you*!"

An involuntary shudder ran through Kuper.

"She was alive!" Kyp continued. "Others saw it. *You* left her there, just the way we left you."

"You're lying," Kuper said at last in a low, thick voice.

"Ask Kort. He saw it —"

"You're making it up!" Kuper roared and stabbed at Kyp. Kyp skittered to one side.

"I swear by the Maker!" he shouted, ducking another slash.

Kuper took a step forward, looming almost overtop Kyp. "You're lying!"

"I swear by Great Crow. I swear by the First Nest and the First Brood, and all the Crows that came after. It's true. Confirm it with others if you want."

Kuper continued to advance. Kyp scrambled backward through the juniper, to the edge of the mountaintop. "You killed Kalum. You attacked the flock. And for what? For doing *exactly* the same thing that you did."

Kuper stood. Buffeted by the struggle within. A tremor shook him, and his eyes stared blankly into space.

Kyp seized the moment, turned and leaped into the air.

"I'll kill you!" Kuper snarled and flew straight after him.

The incline on this side of the mountaintop was sheer, plunging past crumbling shale precipices far, far down into the river valley below. When your wings are injured, you can still fold them and fly after a fashion. You lose mobility but you gain speed. Kyp tucked his wings in and flew the way a stone flies. He simply dropped, falling fast and picking up speed. Following behind, Kuper realized that at that speed there would soon be no way to stop. Kyp shot past a rocky outcrop. The valley bottom rushed up to greet him. He opened his wings slightly, hoping to slow his fall. His right wing immediately screamed with pain and crumpled. He spun to the right — and the river was *there*, right in front of him. Kuper spread his wings, banked into a tight turn and curled back up, but Kyp hit the surface like a hailstone fired by the Maker herself. Spray and foam leaped up and sucked him under. Down he dove, deep, his speed propelling him to the gravelly bottom. The cold shocked him but he managed to keep his beak closed. In the canyon above, Kuper turned tight circles, scanning the river. Waiting.

Kyp remained under, the freezing water numbing him, the current pushing him along, over gravel beds, against rocks, past tangled, submerged roots. He glanced behind and saw something brown and large approaching fast, bouncing, swinging, rolling through the water. As it hurtled at him, he grabbed it, clung to it, felt crumbling wood beneath his talons. Lungs bursting, he fought to press himself close to the coarse bark.

Below the water, the world is reversed. The shimmering surface becomes your sky. The world of fish, rocks and weeds flickers by, blue gray and soothing. The rushing water hisses and whispers, "Stay. Stay and I will tell you stories you have never heard. Stay." But if you listen too long to the stories the water tells, you will never breathe air again.

Kyp clung to the floating log. When there was no air remaining in his lungs, he crawled to the surface and threw himself down. He retched, coughed and at last drew a long, cold, clear breath.

And then, darkness.

chapter 8

Kyp awoke.

The sun warmed and dried his back. Wind ruffled the feathers along the nape of his neck. How long had he been wherever he was? He raised his head, looked about, then had to let it drop again. The world rocked and wobbled. How long had he lain there? Had he been asleep two days? Three days? More?

He tried to rise, his wing shot fire. He tried to recall where he was and what had happened. Then he heard Kalum's voice telling him, "You have to find her."

"How?" he asked again wearily and fell back to sleep.

From the darkness of his own thoughts, he heard water murmur. He woke once again, the sun slanting from another direction. Another sunrise? His throat was bone dry and his tongue clung to the top of his beak. He dipped his head over the edge of the log and drank. He glanced at the river's high, crumbling banks that rose on either side. How far had he traveled? Sandstone bluffs loomed close and then slipped past. Clumps of gray-green willow sprang from the vertical stone walls. Ancient, rough-skinned poplars stretched over the river, trailing drooping branches in the current. He thrust his head under the surface to clear his mind. The water ran warmer here than it had close to the mountains, and muddier.

Suddenly the log jarred as it caught on a rock, spun loose and became trapped in the stringy roots and reeds of a shallow stretch of gravel and still backwater. Kyp fought to stand on shaky legs and hopped from the driftwood onto a thin branch that projected from the clay bank. Ants worried their way up and down the plant, tending aphids. Alarmed by the intruder, they rushed along the branch to confront Kyp, who plucked them up and ate them, gradually feeling strength returning to him.

Slowly he hopped up the bush from one bobbling branch to another, until finally he reached the crest of the embankment. He stepped out onto grass and, blinking, surveyed the landscape. The mountains had disappeared. Rolling prairie stretched as far as his eyes could see. Sunbaked sedge, smoky-colored sage and the occasional stunted rosebush spread to the horizon. The sky arced above, a dusty pale blue. It was entirely new territory to Kyp. No landmark distinguished any part from any other part. His right wing was suddenly wracked by a spasm, and the pain nearly made him black out. He hopped back down to the safety of the riverbank.

He drew another long drink from the river. Where to go? The log shimmied in the water, pushed by the current but still captured in reeds, but it wasn't an answer. Kyp knew he had been lucky that no hungry raccoon or vulture had come upon him while he lay in open view.

Behind him, and a short hop up the bank, was a Crow-sized hole burrowed just beneath an overhanging lip of grass. Kyp cautiously approached it and peered in. As far back as he could see, there was nothing but dust, the odd gnarled root and darkness. He drew a deep breath. There was the clean scent of crumbling clay, sand, willow — nothing else. He stuck his head in and — though it was forbidden by law and flew in the face of good sense — stepped inside. The wind had scattered leaves and twigs along the ground, and they crunched under his talons as he paced slowly ahead.

The darkness enfolded him. He sniffed again and called softly. Nothing. At last he turned around, curled up and studied the surroundings from the tunnel entrance. From this vantage, well above the river, he could look across the water and down the bank in either direction. He saw the waterlogged piece of driftwood wobble once, slowly pull clear of the branches it had been entangled in and spin back into the current. Moments later it disappeared around a bend downstream.

Chapter 9

Those were long days that Kyp spent healing, and during that time he learned to live like a groundling. He slept in his adopted burrow for much of the day. He dragged up rocks, bush branches and dried thistle stalks to hide the entrance. He crept to the river in the morning to drink and clean himself. He took what food he could find and returned with it to the den. To crouch. To think. To sleep, if possible.

In his fight with Kuper, Kyp had cracked a bone below the shoulder of his right wing, and that would take some time to mend. Just as seriously, though, he had lost or snapped several primary wing feathers. Until he molted and new feathers came in, even if his broken bone mended quickly, there could be no flying any distance. He would have to settle in, stay put and wait.

There was food to be had, but not much. Bugs from the river and tiny green frogs. The odd worm. Scavenge sometimes washed up along the shore, but more often than not it had already been picked clean. When his hunger grew too fierce, Kyp limped through the prairie and plucked up startled grasshoppers as they sprang from grass blades. He knew all too well that a wounded Crow on the ground would be irresistible to a passing hawk or owl, so he limited his visits. For the most part, he stayed hungry and lost weight.

Time dragged. The hole was hot and dusty most of the time, and damp and muddy when it rained. He felt cramped and bored, and he longed to stretch his wings. He tried not to think of the past. When night fell, though, he would see his flock again, dying, their bodies gathered in piles beneath the Gathering Tree. He flew slowly over the prone bodies, searching. Kuper would loom up out of the darkness and taunt him. Then suddenly Kalum would appear next to him on a branch, fix him with a stern, steady gaze and say, "You have to find her."

One day as he was resting, the heat beyond the den rising in lingering, even waves, Kyp raised his head and saw the sleek, flattened face of a snake slowly lifting through the haze. A hole is a hard thing to enter if something bars the way. Kyp had to become that thing. He sat up, his feathers flaring. The snake coiled, head swaying. Its glittering eyes fixed on Kyp. Kyp didn't wait, but struck first. The snake dodged, recoiled and lunged. Kyp snapped left with his beak and caught it on the side of its head, sending it tumbling down the slope. The snake recovered, hesitated, then, deciding that Kyp wasn't *quite* as injured as it had assumed, slipped round a rock and out of sight, as quiet in its leaving as in its coming.

Kyp piled more rocks and brush in front of the hole.

Molt came. He shed and replaced his old feathers. To keep foxes and coyotes from becoming aware of his presence, he was careful to tuck all the old feathers at the back of the den.

At last his bone mended. He flexed his wing muscles and could feel that they had grown weak from lack of use.

One morning as the sun was creeping through a cloud-rimmed, far-off horizon, Kyp clambered to the top of the ravine, sprang to the crown of a small bush and spread his wings. He felt the cool morning air coil around and beneath them. The prairie grasses bowed and bobbed, the wind gently stroking each blade. Which direction to go? His bones had mended slowly, but the spirit takes even longer. When you are lost even to yourself, where can you go to get found?

Kyp made a decision, brought his wings down in a quick, clean stroke and flew.

He wasn't yet strong enough to travel fast or far, so he stayed low, flying from one identifiable landmark to the next. That flowering bush. That ridge. That pile of rocks. For the most part he stayed close to the meandering river valley. Cover was easier to find, and there was water to drink in this otherwise dry land. Able to forage more widely now, he ate better — salamanders, shrews, gophers and voles, ripening berries and water skimmers.

He stopped often to rest, and he preened and cleaned his feathers fanatically. He chose his stops carefully and kept a watchful eye open. The prairie is home to the red-tailed hawk, and a lone Crow is always at risk. The hawk sits on his high perch in the clouds and stares down. Things he likes he follows, quiet as the prairie grass grows. The Crow that doesn't keep his top eye open today is tomorrow's meal.

Kyp's evening roost was wherever he halted when night fell. A thin, sun-scorched tree. A cliff along the river. At first he flew only short distances — the fever still returned if he overworked his wings. As his muscles strengthened and healed, he was able to go farther, faster.

At night, when he perched, the broad cover of the vast night sky and the firefly-bright flickering stars were his only company. The wind murmuring through the grass was all the conversation he shared.

chapter 10

The prairie is wide and seemingly without end, but eventually, after many days of flight, it fell away and was replaced by a gently rolling land of wooded hills and shaded marshes. Kyp glided in lazy curves through the sloping valleys until he arrived at the westernmost edge of a long, sandy lakeshore. The lake itself was immense and home to any number of birds. Gulls skimmed the surface and called loudly to one another. Ducks and loons paddled in the reeds. A large-headed kingfisher perched in a tree overhanging the lake and stared intently into the depths. What secrets did he see etched in the lake bottom? Occasionally he dropped in head first to find out.

Kyp clung to a stone outcrop above the shimmering water. His reflection stared back, a leaner, more ragged Crow than the one who had arrived at the Gathering Tree in the spring. Then, through his shimmering reflection, he spied something else. A fat, lithe trout wriggled out from under a rock, rose and delicately sucked a water strider from the surface. Without thinking, Kyp dropped from his perch, more a leap than a dive. His talons bit deep into the fish, and all at once he held it squirming and twisting, threatening to drag him under. Kyp swept his wings back, lifted the fish and himself free of the water. High into the air he flew and over the shore. There, he released the writhing fish.

The fish spun head over tail and landed with a loud, wet, heavy smack upon the rocks. Kyp curled back to where the fish lay prone, hungrily looking forward to his next meal. But before he could return, he heard a rush of air and, as he turned, was surprised to see another Crow cut between him and his fish. The Crow swooped in, lowered his legs and grabbed. With that, Kyp's meal disappeared down the river valley.

Chapter 11

This fish thief flew well and had a healthy head start, but he was carrying scavenge after all, so Kyp flew faster.

The Thief glanced back and noticed Kyp swiftly approaching. He drew his wings together and plummeted head first into a thicket of maple and thistle. Down through the brush, past the tree branches, almost to ground level, where the bushes and thorns are pushed aside in narrow pathways, where rabbits and fox hide and deer run. Under branches and through reeds, the fish thief sped, emerging eventually along the river. He looped out over the current, glanced back — and saw Kyp. Still following. Closer now.

"This one," the Thief thought with grudging admiration, "*this one* can fly." The fish was starting to weigh him down, but he shifted it in his talons and followed the river until he arrived at one of the larger human roosts. There, he flew directly at a wall of the roost. Just when it seemed as though he must crash, the wall magically divided and slid open. Now he was inside — and the humans were barking and howling in fear and confusion, throwing up their paws. The Thief kept flying. Humans lunged after him, threw things — but the Thief was agile, laughing to himself as he imagined what the other Crow must have thought when he flew through the wall. Then he heard a different kind of disturbance among the humans. He craned his head around — and saw Kyp deftly navigating through the teeming, frenzied humans. And he was closer.

The Thief gave an exasperated snort, gripped his fish more tightly, tucked his head in and swooped around a corner, directly at another wall. It split as well, and the Thief shot out.

Outside, the Thief tried to put some distance between himself and Kyp. For all his efforts, though, Kyp was still pursuing him and was getting closer.

Every Crow who stakes territory has the advantage of familiarity with the terrain. The Thief considered his options and then plunged into a steep dive down a ravine. At the bottom of the gulch, a trickle of water drained into a narrow tunnel. The Thief entered the tunnel's mouth at full speed, but within moments Kyp was in as well.

What Kyp couldn't know was that on the other side of the hill, the tunnel emptied onto a stream. Not a stream of water, but a stream of a different and deadlier kind — a stream of humans in their moving boxes traveling at tremendous speed. You come out head first into that stream and you die. The Thief had used this as an escape before. When he left the tunnel mouth, he immediately curled straight up high above the hill and the humans — and then stopped to look back.

Kyp emerged moments later, unaware, and found himself directly in the path of an onrushing human box. "Death," the Thief murmured. "Snip, snap — this Crow is done." But Kyp didn't try to outfly the human box, and he didn't panic either. Instead he dove flat, flew low and slithered right between the dark, churning paws of the rumbling moving box. Then he snapped up on the other side like water fired from a geyser.

The Thief cursed, turned and flew — but because he had stopped to watch, there was now almost no distance between the two Crows.

The Thief could feel Kyp's breath on his feathers. He flung the fish down, hoping that Kyp would stop to pick it up, but Kyp kept after him. Finally, the Thief realized there was no point flying anymore and dropped to a barren patch of gravel and sand.

Kyp landed beside him. "Who are you?" he demanded.

"Katakata ru Kamu, traveler, outcast and Thief," I told him, because it was I who had led him on this chase.

And as I spoke to him, I was panting like the newest newling returned from its first flight. "I snatch the fish from the osprey's claws," I wheezed, "the frog from the heron's beak. Who," I gasped, "in the name of Great Crow, are you?"

"Kyp ru Kurea ru Kinaar," he told me, and I was pleased to see that he was, at least, breathing as hard as I was.

"You're bigger than me," I told him, "and, it would seem faster. Take my life if you want it."

"Why would I do that?" he asked, seeming genuinely surprised. Then he flew back, retrieved his fish, returned and dropped it between us. "Have some, and Good eating," he said simply. And he looked at me as if to say, "How badly can you have wanted that trout?" Then he teetered, tipped and fell over.

That's when I realized that he was sick. *Sick.*

It changed me, you understand? Seeing him on the ground, and me standing before him with my beak open. He flew like that, and he wasn't even flying with all his feathers straight. "Maker," I told myself. "Maker, from this day forward, don't *ever* let me boast to anyone that I can fly. If *this one* can fly like that, and catch *me*, in my own territory, when he's not even healthy, Great Crow, what can I expect from him when he's well?"

I tore off a small strip of fish and fed it to him, a bit at a time. When he had revived enough, he rose to his talons and we shared the meal we had both worked so hard to get.

chapter 12

When he recovered, he explained that he hadn't flown full out like that since he had contracted the fever and broken his wing. I told him not to say another thing. If he could fly like that, I said, when he hadn't fully recovered, he didn't have to explain anything to anyone.

After we had eaten our fill, he asked where my flock was. I told him I had no flock, no Clan, no Family.

"Has the Plague caught them as well?" he asked. I replied yes, but said I couldn't tell him any more than that unless he had more time to listen than the time it takes to eat a fish. He said he had nothing but time. So we settled on a nearby branch, and I told him.

"The beginning of everything bad often starts first in our dreams. Our old Chooser, Katratu ru Kamu, dreamed that a flock of skeletons flew through the sky, the wind whistling through their bones, then perched on the tree alongside our Family. 'Good eating,' she called to them, but the skeletons simply turned their eyeless skulls, stared with their blank sockets and gave no reply. Shrugging, Katratu returned to her meal, but she quickly realized that no matter how much she ate, she remained hungry. Soon she saw why. Everything she ate traveled past her beak, down her throat and then spilled out her ribs — she had been transformed into a skeleton as well.

"When she woke, she relayed this dream to the other Elders. Some said it meant this, and others said it meant that. Some said that sometimes a dream is just a dream. But a half moon later, a hawk stooped and caught Katratu, and though she fought, her wounds proved too severe. She struggled for three days before her spirit abandoned her body and flew to the Maker. She was my great-aunt, a respected Elder, and canny in the ways of dealing with other Crows. Even disagreeable ones. If someone was upset, she could comfort them. If there was an argument, she knew how to crack the nut that would solve it. She knew *all* the stories, all their meanings and all their origins. And she knew how to keep the flock together.

"All that changed when, following her death, the flock chose someone else to Choose. The new Chooser — Katakilu ru Karu — was different in large and small ways. He and some of the Elders held strong opinions about what the Maker wanted and didn't want. Every time you returned to the roost, it seemed they had invoked new rules. Especially rules about how to deal with the human.

"There had always been commandments regarding the human, but the flock had had some recent bad experiences. Some of the flock had been caught in traps set by the human. Some had died in those traps. One of those was my mother. Katakilu and the Elders decided that the flock must avoid all things human. Any contact, even the most minor, must be followed by prayer and purification.

"Well. That season, there was drought. Hot beyond hot, every day. So hot you wanted to pluck out your feathers, lay them on the ground and travel about naked as the day you first hatched. Salvage so hard to come by, there were days when you had only the vague memory of food to savor. Humans, though — humans had altered the river so it flowed near their roosts. There — where the humans lived — every day was spring. Everything was green and growing ripe and lovely. Everywhere else, everything was brown, burnt, dry, dusty. And where were we forced to roost because we were supposed to avoid all things human? In the middle of the dust. In the middle of the heat.

"I grumbled for a while and asked myself, 'Is it right? Is it right for the humans to take everything, to take *my own mother* even, and then not share their salvage?' I asked myself those questions, and my answer was 'No.' So I went where the human was. I ate, and I said, 'Maker, if this is wrong, show me.'

"But it wasn't the Maker who caught me returning. It was our Chooser, Katakilu. He called out for a Judgment. The Judgment convened, and the Elders commanded me, "Katakata, purify and pray, and you will be forgiven. Purify and pray, say you were in error, and everything will be good again." I refused. As far as the Chooser and the Elders were concerned, that was the wrong answer.

"They Banished me, struck my name and drove me from the roost. They told me never to come back. Never. That's a long, long flight.

"So. I traveled north. That's good land there. Plenty of trees and good eating. But being on your own — it's hard. To rebel is one thing, to *choose* to be alone. To be *sent* away, *Banished*, and to know that it's forever — that's another. I had no one to perform watch for me when I drank. No one to provide warning when I roosted. And up north, there are plenty of owls and eagles, and everything else that likes Crow at every meal.

"At first I cursed the Chooser, but I had a lot of time to think. I learned how to take what I needed and get away quick. I learned to thrive up north during the summer, and then when my old flock flew south, I moved to where our flock traditionally held the spring Gathering, and there I lived off human salvage through the winter. There's a special kind of knowledge that comes from living through the cold. It's not just making do for yourself and finding a warm corner when the wind comes. There's time to think things through when there's nothing to keep you company but snow, ice, sleet and a lot of other cold things that can't talk or do anything but frost your beak and make you miserable.

"I know I'm not perfect. Part of what happened between my flock and me, I built into the nest. But no one can cut me out of the Maker's sight. She knows my name, she's counted my feathers, and she knows my story.

"This year, toward the end of the summer, I flew back to the old Gathering grounds. The flock would be making its move south and I thought I might catch sight of the last few stragglers from afar. I suppose I wanted to see if I remembered who was who. Instead, there they were, the Crows who drove me out, splayed on the ground. The sickness must have struck them all at once. Maybe sixty of them. For all their prayer and purification, the Maker had abandoned them. The flock of skeletons my great-aunt had dreamed of had arrived, and there was no shaking their bony talons from the roost.

"I thought as I looked at the bodies of those who had held Judgment on me that I would feel some satisfaction, but I didn't. I just felt sad."

Kyp listened patiently while I talked — and I talked for quite a long time. I hadn't had anyone to unburden myself to since my Banishment. When I was finished, he just nodded. Then, without saying anything about it at all, we began to fly.

That was the beginning of my flight with Kyp ru Kurea ru Kinaar. In addition to being the most able flier I have ever seen, he had other talents, as I soon learned. He had a sharp eye for finding good eating and fresh salvage. Bushes thick with berries. Ponds alive with minnows. He saw them first, every time.

There's a special knack for finding a roost — I don't have it. I can *find* a roost — an uncomfortable one, that the wind screams through and the frost crusts up on. But Kyp had that skill. Kyp could fly and look and fly and look, then suddenly select a roost, and I wouldn't know why he picked it. But the roost he chose would provide shelter from hawks, it would be near food and water, and it would be comfortable. Choosing a roost is a gift, and he had it.

So that's how we would do it. We would rise each morning, feed, stretch our wings and set out. We flew slowly, talked a little — or at least I did — to pass the time.

Flying alone teaches you about the world. Even more than that, it teaches you about yourself — but it is a kind of learning bought with silence. I had flown alone so long there were stories I had rehearsed and was eager to share. I told Kyp some of the old tales I hadn't heard since I sat in a nest, peered over the rim and looked down from the tree. It was good to hear those tales spoken aloud again — even if it was only my tongue and beak that offered them roost. Great Crow and the First Tree. Great Crow and the World Snake. The Long Flight. Death Born. Just recollecting these stories was a rare pleasure. We flew for some distance before I realized that I was receiving none in return.

Kyp was an extraordinary flight partner, no question. But he was a Crow who flew with his beak shut. Some days we flew from first to last sixth and nothing more than "Good eating" passed his beak.

One evening, we set down to roost and I told him, "Dreams mean something, Cousin."

He looked at me and said "Sometimes," which was his way of telling me he didn't want to talk about it. Then he began preening. Like there was nothing more to be said on that subject.

"So?" I asked, meaning So, what stories have made you?

He didn't look up from what he was doing. "So what?" he replied, very sharp.

"So, what dreams have you been sent?"

"No dreams. I'm a pretty sound sleeper."

"*Everyone* dreams," I persisted.

"Not me," he retorted, and he didn't quite yawn, although that was the tone he used, like this conversation was beyond boring.

"Cousin," I said, "please don't insult my intelligence. If you want me to shut up, I will. You want me to keep my ideas to myself? I can do that, too. But I roost in the same tree as you. If you talk to yourself, I hear it, so I *know* you dream."

He snapped his head around, angry now. "Do you know," he said very deliberately, "the story of the Crow who asked the same question too often?" And by that he meant I'd said more than enough, but I told him.

"Do I? Ho, that was one of the first I ever heard, when I was just a little ball of down with nothing but mites to keep me company in the nest. Every day little Kedu asks why? *Why* have we beaks? *Why* have we backs? *Why* do we sleep with our heads to one side? His father says, 'Kedu, you will have to learn to be quiet or you will go hungry.'

"But little Kedu keeps asking why. He goes to the

bear, asks, '*Why* do you growl?' Goes to Raccoon, asks, '*Why* do you fish?' His mother says, 'Kedu, you must learn to be quiet or you will never find a mate.'

"But little Kedu keeps asking. One day he comes upon Coyote as he's leading a flock of partridges to his den. Kedu says, '*Why* are you doing that?' Coyote says to him, 'I am a teacher and these are my students. They are all following me to my den, where I will teach them how to be quiet.' Kedu says, 'Ho, perfect! That's just the thing I need to learn!' So Kedu crawled into Coyote's lair, and you won't hear any questions from little Kedu anymore, and snip, snap, that's the end.

"But, Cousin, *I've* been into the coyote's den, and I have taught the coyote a thing or two about how to sing. I have been in, come out, and that coyote is still holding his lip going ow, ow, owwwww. Ow ow owww!"

Despite himself, Kyp laughed, and I told him, "Like Kedu, I'm going to keep asking you."

He sighed a deep sigh, like I was the heaviest thing he ever carried. Then he shook his head and began.

"I dream of the Kinaar. That's all. It's nothing."

I shook my head, too. "Dreams, Cousin, are never nothing."

"Maybe that's *your* experience with dreams."

And then he flew. I lifted my wings and followed him. East, always east.

Eventually we stopped for the night. As usual, Kyp found a spot that was safe and protected from the wind and rain, a small pear tree wedged between two big spreading beeches. We performed three circuits, but there weren't any humans nearby, so we settled on a sheltered, broad branch near the trunk. Kyp had outdone himself in his selection of a roost, because though it was late in the season, the pears still hung from the tree, thin skinned, soft and wonderfully sweet nearest the core. There were so many that we could even be careless with them. We ate our fill — much more than our fill really — and soon were throwing half-eaten cores to the ground. Many of the pears had been sitting a little long on the branch, and eventually I could feel they were making me light-headed.

"Kyp," I said after having consumed several of these over-ripe pears, "conversation is a bird that requires two wings to fly."

He scrunched up his eyes, shut his beak tighter and gave me his death stare. I ignored it, snatched another pear and kept on going.

"We've flown together how long now? Since the beginning of lake country. You know everything about me from the time I struggled out of the shell.

You know about my Clan. You know why I flew solo. You know what I've done since I was Banished. You know what I like to eat, when I like to sleep and the names of all my favorite aunts. *When*," I asked, "do I hear *your* stories?"

He didn't have any stories, he told me.

"I don't believe that." I shook my head — then stopped. Shaking my head made the tree wiggle a little too much. "Why east?" I asked once things had steadied sufficiently. "Why that direction? Why not north, or south?"

No reason. He just said that each morning when he was on his own, he woke and asked the world what direction he should take. Nothing provided him with a clear answer, so when he saw the sun rising, he said to himself, "That's the way — east."

He tossed a core to the ground and plucked another pear from the tree. "Do you want to go another way?"

I told him no. "East is good," I said. "I have no complaints with east."

We devoured more pears, and these pears, these pears were *some* pears, let me tell you. I probably like pears as much as the next Crow, but *these* pears — I could have eaten a hundred of them. Juicy. Tangy. Thirst quenching. How, I asked myself, could any fruit be so delicious? Even the peel seemed especially beautiful: bright red and gold. Delicately dappled. The blended colors of a brilliant autumn sunset captured in one neat and compact oval. Why had I never noticed that about a pear before?

Finally I drew my attention away from the exceptional pear and stared at Kyp. "Are you searching for something in particular?"

He didn't reply for a long time, so I repeated the question. He said he didn't know.

I was past being cautious. I told him that if he didn't have the courtesy to answer me politely, at least he could tell me the truth. He protested that he wasn't lying, but I said if he could claim that after flying on his own for an entire summer, then flying with me all this time, he hadn't the faintest notion why we were heading east, he was either lying to me or was the simplest newling.

All at once, he was telling me everything. About the sickness and the Crow who wanted revenge. About Kym and the humans who captured her. He didn't know why he was traveling east, he knew only that the Chooser for his flock told him to find her, and he felt he had to, but he didn't know where to start.

We both grew quiet for a long time.

I placed my pear down gently on the branch — it could have been my sixteenth or seventeenth. "Kyp," I told him, "I'll help you. I'll help you find her."

"How?" he asked, and I can't recall when I've

heard such hopelessness expressed in one word.

"I don't know," I told him, "but I promise you this. Before we have finished traveling, you and I, we will have found her."

"Don't promise that," he said quietly.

"I *am* promising that."

"Don't."

"I *am*," I repeated. "Because you, Kyp ru Kurea, are a Crow with a big, big heart. Any other Crow would have killed me. *Any* other Crow! Why, if *I* had met me, and I had stolen that fish from me, and I was as hungry as you were, and sick, and then I had chased me down through the forest and the humans' roost and all of that — *I* would have killed me." I found I was becoming confused, so I returned to the essential point. "But you didn't. You" — I tapped him on his chest — "didn't."

Kyp just gnawed on a pear, then tossed it. "The Maker does strange things," he said at last. "Why make someone like Kym, who can understand the human the way she does, only to have her taken by the human?"

I found this question so curious that a strange chill ran through me and I felt my feathers rise. Suddenly I was wide, wide awake. "Say that again," I said.

"Say what?" he asked.

"About Kym. About Kym and the humans."

Kyp could see that something was bothering me. "I just said, why make someone like Kym, who can understand the human the way she does, only to have her taken by the human."

"What do you mean by that?"

"She loved humans," he said, "and used to watch them all the time, regardless of all the extra prayer and purification it caused her. She knew things about them that no other Crow ever has. Even knew how to speak to them a little, in their own tongue."

There are moments when the Maker is right *there* on the branch, so close you can feel her. I shook my head to clear it. The chill was still running through me, stronger even than before, but I had to make sure it wasn't just the pear speaking.

"Kyp, listen to me," I said. "Earlier in the summer. Before I met you. I was perched by the lake, hungry. I said to myself, why not fly over by the human trackway and see if there is any scavenge there. It can offer dangerous feeding, because the human boxes race so quickly — if you get too involved with feeding and don't keep your eyes open, it's easy to get hit. And of course there are always hawks prowling above, but like I said, I was hungry. Away I flew. Sure enough, there was a dead porcupine off to the side of the trackway. A magpie was already feeding. I looked around, didn't see anything else. 'He's just a magpie,' I said to myself, and I landed.

'Good eating,' I greeted him, nodded and started to eat, too. The magpie complained and fussed, said this and that, but I didn't really pay much attention. After all, he was a magpie — what's more natural than for a magpie to complain? We both ate our fill and retired to a bush to preen. He'd settled down and was behaving a little better — as far as a magpie is able to behave. I told him a story, he told me a story. That's the way things are among birds who talk, Kyp."

Kyp just flicked a wing at me, urging me to get on with it. "What has this to do with —"

"Hold on a moment. This magpie told me *he* was taken by humans, too."

Suddenly Kyp sat up straighter. I continued. "He said he was placed inside something — he described it as a swallow's nest made of stone — and carried a great distance, along with other birds. But when the humans went to take him out of the nest-thing, something fell to the ground, broke and he escaped. So he was making his way home, going west. To tell you the truth, I didn't listen all that closely to everything he said, because he was a magpie, after all. Half of what he was saying I couldn't understand, and, anyways, who can trust a magpie? But at one point he mentioned that there was one Crow among those who were captured, a female, who tried to speak with the humans in their own language."

Now Kyp's feathers rose. We perched there on that branch, and as the wind slithered and slipped through the dry leaves, they shivered and hissed. Finally he opened his beak. "Where had he escaped from?"

"I don't know. East. A long way east. He said he'd come from a huge human nesting ground out that way. Bigger, much bigger, than anything he'd ever seen. When he escaped, he just flew and flew. He'd been on the wing for some time when we met."

Kyp sat like a frozen thing, and I sat there, too, thinking. Sometimes life is so strange it stuns you.

"Do you think it's her?" I asked finally.

"It has to be," Kyp replied slowly. "A Crow captured. Female. Someone who speaks human. How many Crows like that can there be?"

My head spun. The Maker plays a complicated game of tag with us sometimes. She touches us lightly and flies off, and who has wings big enough to keep up? Why had I met Kyp? Why had I met the magpie? How could these things happen and *not* be connected in some way? I wondered how Kyp must feel. This Kym, somewhere out east, among humans, somewhere in some human nesting ground, captured. Great Crow, what a tangled flight through the thorny underbrush it all was. But when I glanced over at Kyp, he seemed happier than I had ever seen him.

"What?" I asked. I didn't know what I was asking exactly. Maybe What are you thinking? Or maybe What — do you have something else to tell me? But I believe mostly I was asking him What in all that I told you makes you happy?

He just said, "She's alive. She's still alive."

I nodded. "And we'll find her."

We fell asleep in the crook of that pear tree, an immense pile of half-eaten pear cores littering the ground beneath us. We slept till the sun was high the next day, flew to a nearby stream and drank for a long time.

When we'd finished, I asked which way.

"East is where your magpie came from," he said.

And off we flew.

Now some of you Crows can live on talk, and some of you can live on flight, but I'm one who needs drink and food and plenty of it, and right now I need to stretch as well. Let us break, Cousins.

part two

chapter 13

Draw in. Those of you on the outer branches, draw in.

The wind has picked up, and my words will be lifted and scattered along with the crystals of frost and the remaining leaves of this tree. Draw in, listen and take what warmth you can from the flock around you.

Cousins, a story is a record, and for some of you it will be the only record you will ever have of those who were near to you and are now gone. Even more than that, a story is a sacred opportunity. We are, every Crow son and daughter of us, blown through the storm that is our life's journey. Who are we here on these branches but fortunate survivors? And yet there are those who have shared our journey and have not been so lucky. With this story, they are made immortal. Each time the story is retold, they will live again. This is a special blessing passed from the Maker's beak to ours.

So now, draw in.

It was the first gentle beginnings of fall. Leaves turned color, and the rains came. Kyp and I flew together, but as we traveled, we discovered with each perch we made that the Plague had flown ahead of us and had scattered death and fear wherever it roosted. Many Families, like Kyp's, had taken flight and fled south. For some, sickness had killed more than half, and all that remained were bones, talons and feathers in the wind. Some Clans were diminished but retained a core group. Almost none had stayed to roost and nest and raise chicks. In any case, we met nearly no Crows. The few we did spot kept their distance and shouted only terse responses to our questions, afraid that we might approach too close and carry the disease. On the odd occasion, we spoke with a solitary magpie or jay. It was from them that we received any real news, what we could decipher and translate, but none of them carried the slightest rumor of a Crow who could talk to humans.

Then, one day, following a long flight, we roosted in a thick grove of beech and elm. It was nearing the final sixth and the brooding shadows stretched long, lean and dark. Kyp was taking his own sweet time to sort his feathers, as he always did, when all at once he froze and whispered, "Owl."

I scanned the grove. "Where?"

"There," he croaked, "in that fat oak. Halfway up, near the crook. Feeding."

I saw nothing. I searched each tree more carefully — and spotted it. A big adult. Gray and tan, with a black and white flecked breast and a face like a withered knot in a craggy tree trunk. Pushed in, pushed back, a big bushy ridge of feathers all around, cold evil yellow eyes peering out from within that dark, hollow dip of a face. It was tearing up a rabbit that it held firmly to the branch with its massive talons.

We sat quietly a moment, then I asked Kyp, "Can you fly?"

He turned to me, puzzled, and repeated the question. "Can I fly?"

"Are your wings fit?" I asked impatiently.

"Sure. Yes."

"Good," I said. "We can play tag."

Kyp was still asking what I meant by "tag" when I flew from our tree. I went directly at that owl and hit it on the left side of its head with the back of my right talon. Its surprise must have been considerable because it nearly toppled from its perch. Then it regained its balance, stuck its neck out like a snake and hissed.

"Good eating," I wished it, then spun around and swung back. The owl dropped its rabbit and was after me in an instant. Kyp stared at me, big eyed, as I approached with that livid owl in pursuit.

"Tag," I called. "*You're* it, Kyp!"

I dove through the branches and under a spray of ivy. Kyp quickly slung himself off the perch as that owl went after him. Then something happened that I can only describe as magic. Kyp flew as Great Crow must have flown when he felt particularly lively. He darted under branches and looped back through clusters of nettle. He rolled and curled, faked and feinted, doubled back on himself till that poor, weary owl didn't know which direction was up or what he was chasing. It was, in every way, a thing of beauty to watch.

When we met again, it was growing dark, and a purple-gray mist had settled over the valley. A hushed, delicate rain was falling. We'd designated a chestnut tree as our alternate roost, and Kyp was still puffing as he flew in, favoring his left side. That right wing, I thought, still needs a bit more exercise.

"Here," I said, holding the owl's rabbit out to him. "Well flown! You have a genuine talent, you know that?"

He gulped air and snatched a portion of rabbit from my talons, a bit roughly, I thought. Then he looked at me sternly and snapped, "You didn't have to do that."

"Do what?" I asked, a little unclearly perhaps. I was enjoying my meal, and my beak was still half full.

"Put us at risk like that. We can find things for ourselves."

"*Find* things for ourselves?" I snorted and held up the salvage in my right talon. "Is *this* tasty and delicious, or not? Would you rather our big-eyed friend the *owl* dined on it? The Maker didn't place us on Earth to merely '*find* things for ourselves.' '*Find* things for ourselves?' What earthly good is that?" I tore another strip off the scavenge. "Are we dogs that we should *sniff* out our food or snakes that we should slither into holes after it? Is a Crow an eagle? A hawk? A falcon? To *steal* something, Cousin, and to steal it clean, is a gift, and a sacred thing. The Maker made the cormorant to dive after minnows, the swallow to capture mosquitoes, and the Maker made us, Cousin, to *think* for a living." I wrenched another bite from the scavenge. "Just consider Great Crow."

"Exactly," he replied and swallowed. "*Look* at Great Crow. Clever. Independent. Self-sufficient. Able to do anything he wanted. He didn't rely on the efforts of anyone else — and *that*'s what made him Great Crow."

"Excuse me, Cousin," I protested, "but *you* are confused. Great Crow was Great because he could *see* — and what he *saw* was glorious, blessed opportunity everywhere. Great Crow was the first thief."

"That," Kyp said, shaking his head, "is just blasphemy."

"That is truth! And if the Maker is listening, believe me, she is shaking her head at your woeful, sorry lack of education. Do I have to instruct you? Perch then, and listen. And don't eat all the rabbit while I tutor you." I whet my beak against the branch as I recalled the story. "Think back. Think back through all the layers of yesterdays, all the way to First Times. Everyone remembers them as being particularly blessed. But it wasn't always good eating and a safe roost after. The animals, as you'll remember, became discontented with the Maker. 'Why am I chased all the time?' whined Mouse. 'Why am I ravenous all the time,' growled Weasel, 'and must wear my claws to the nub hunting day and night?' And of course, every animal had its own predicament and complaint. No one was content. Everyone desired what the other had. And the Maker, if you'll remember, decided that enough was enough. And by way of punishment, she took the sun away.

"No sun. Imagine that.

"Mornings without dawn. Evening without end. Every moment dark and getting darker. Cold and growing colder. So now, there were all the animals of the world and nothing but night and stars. The animals huddled close to one another and felt truly wretched. Even the sky felt sorry for itself and began to cry. Its tears fell to Earth frozen.

"The first snow.

"Nobody had ever seen anything like it, nobody knew what it was — but the white, fluffy stuff kept falling. Pretty soon, all the animals were covered from head to claw, shivering and mumbling — what to do? They looked around. Not much point. It was too dark to see anything. Someone way at the back of that crowd suggested, 'Bear's big and has a loud voice. He can go shout at the Maker.'

"'*Shout* at the Maker?' Bear repeated. He covered his snout with his big furry paws and glanced nervously over his shoulder to see if maybe the Maker had been listening. Then he crept away, dug a deep den in the snow and went straight to sleep.

"So the animals shivered a little longer and pretty soon another one suggested, 'What about Wolf? He's strong and he's tireless and he can run down the Maker and make her listen.' And Wolf, imagining what the Maker would think of this, just wailed, 'Why me? Why me?' And he ran away, over the snow, crying. And at night you can still hear him crying at being chosen to confront the Maker.

"So now everyone was *really* cold and still they just sat there, going jj-jj-jj — with their bones rattling about in their bodies and their beaks clacking together, and finally Great Crow got fed up and said, '*I'll* bring the sun back.'

"Everyone cheered, wished him luck and waved him good-bye. Off he flew, but inside he was thinking, *What* am I going to do?

"Through the dark and snow he sailed. He flew south, but it just got colder. Tired, he thought maybe it would be good to stop. He landed, but the snow was so high he sank up to his beak. 'This is no good,' he said, and off he went.

"He stopped in another place but the snow was now so deep he sank over his head. 'This is worse,' he muttered through the snow, and off he went again.

"Finally, he came to the mountains. Here the snow was falling, falling, falling; but off, way off, in one silent, secluded valley, Great Crow saw steam rising. And he thought, What can that be? He landed and the snow was wet and sticky beneath his talons.

"Suddenly he heard the Maker rumble in her great loud voice, 'What are *you* doing here, Great Crow?' And Great Crow, who could make himself appear very abject when he wanted to, groveled convincingly. 'Oh, Maker, thank *goodness* I found you. I've come here to apologize on behalf of all the animals. We *know* we offended you. We *know* we did wrong. And I personally, I want to apologize to you. Please, please forgive me.'

"'That's good, Great Crow, that you feel that way,' the Maker replied gruffly. 'But it's not enough.' The Maker was still really angry.

"'But, Maker, that's not all,' Great Crow continued. 'Falcon is completely contrite. Falcon asked me to bring this message to you. She is sorry beyond sorry. She begs your forgiveness, too.'

"'I hear her apology,' the Maker said, 'but that is not enough.'

"'But there's more, Maker,' Great Crow persisted. 'Beaver, swimming in the water, is thankful for the mud and grime and muck and the hard, green wood that you have provided for her gnawing pleasure. She thanks you and humbly, very humbly apologizes.'

"And so on.

"He just kept apologizing on behalf of every animal he could think of until finally the Maker did what everyone does when an apology stretches on too long. She fell asleep.

"Quietly Great Crow crept over to where he had first seen that steam rising. And what did he find, but deep down, far beneath the ground, a hidden cave where the Maker had concealed Sun Eagle. The feathers of that great glimmering bird flickered and shimmered in the darkness like the red and orange embers of a mighty fire, but he had been placed under some enchantment so powerful that Great Crow couldn't wake him.

"So now Great Crow considered how he was to fetch Sun Eagle back to the animals. The cave was considerably warmer than it was outside, and Great Crow could feel heat radiating off each red and orange quill. Great Crow's talons were still so frozen and numb that he thought, I won't feel it much if I carry him a little way. So he picked up Sun Eagle and off he flew.

"Pretty soon his talons began to thaw, and they started to feel a little bit more than warm. That's not so bad, he thought. Then his talons started to grow entirely too hot. Great Crow shifted Sun Eagle from one talon to the other.

"That worked only until he noticed that his talons were becoming so hot they were smoking. Great Crow said to himself, 'Better put *that* out.' He flew faster, hoping it would extinguish the flames. But the wind loves fire. It blows on the embers, and the flames spring up. Soon Great Crow's talons were completely ablaze, flames licking up his legs to his belly. The pain was excruciating.

"The fire was just beginning to consume Great Crow from the bottom up when he heard a voice next to him. The Maker. 'Great Crow,' she said, 'because you only wished to help others, I am prepared to forgive you this *one* time.' The flames running up Great Crow's legs flickered out, and Sun Eagle abruptly disappeared from Great Crow's talons. 'I will allow Sun Eagle to return to your skies for half the year. The other half of the year he will stay with me and there will be darkness and cold and snow, and then all the animals will remember the apologies you delivered on their behalf.'

"And though the gull's legs are yellow and the owl's legs are white, ours remain black from the time they were burnt stealing the sun.

"And that," I said, finishing my story, "is that. And *there* is your lesson, and let's hope you benefit from it."

The combination of having tricked the owl and having told the story of stealing the sun — one of my favorites — left me feeling just that little bit *too* confident. Which made me fly that one tree too far.

"There's more to the story," I continued. "An ending that doesn't always get told. The journey of Great Crow to find the sun is known by even the smallest chick. Some say the journey took a short time, some say a long time. Me, I think back in First Times, when everything was bigger, even a short time was like a life.

"Many events happened during that long darkness. Through it all, Great Crow traveled alone, and while he did, many waited. Kaynu, Great Crow's First Mate, perched in the darkness and thought her worried thoughts. How will he fly from one place to another? she fretted. What will guide him through the world as he searches for the sun?

"At one point Great Crow glided through the bitter darkness and he noticed a light up ahead and heard a voice. It was Kaynu, his partner. She had changed herself into a star and, though separated from Great Crow forever, helped him find his way. As you know, Kaynu in the old tongue means 'This way.' Every other star in the sky moves, but Kaynu waits in her one place up high. And when we look at that star, it is Kaynu glittering through the darkness and telling us, 'This way, this way, this way.'"

As I said, I felt a little too clever after telling the story, and telling it well — but when I glanced over at Kyp as he sat there, feathers askew, dripping rain, I realized what a foolish, thoughtless mistake I had made. I realized he was thinking of this Kym he had spoken of, and I bitterly regretted telling that portion of the tale. Sometimes, I have to confess, my beak has a life of its own.

Kyp carefully placed his piece of rabbit down on the branch, turned to me and said, "I understand stories are sacred. I understand they have their place on the tree. But from now on, do me this favor. Don't tell me any more stories that end in failure. I haven't got room in my life for that. I can't think that way anymore." And he flew off up the hill into the woods and the mist and the drizzle.

I sat there alone. I said "All right" to the empty place on the branch where he'd perched, and after that, I stopped telling him stories of that sort. But I never told him what I thought, and that is that stories aren't just things we share to pass the time on nights when the roost is uncomfortable or the wind a little strong. Stories are the food our souls eat. And the saddest stories are the medicines our souls need to become stronger.

I cached the rabbit at the base of a nearby tree and roosted for the night. The rabbit should have provided us with a meal the next day as well, but when I woke, I felt something prickly run up and down my back, like someone was watching me. My first thought was, the owl! We should have flown farther. I whipped my head around. There, one tree over, perched in the crook of an oak, three solemn, bony Crows sat, staring.

"Good eating," said the tall one on the left and nodded.

Chapter 14

The others said nothing. "The wind under your wings," Kyp replied. He must have silently returned during the night and perched beside me.

I didn't say anything, but dropped to the forest floor and huddled closer to the remains of our rabbit. There were three of them and only two of us. As small as they were, though, I was pretty sure I could take the bunch of them on my own. They looked like the smallest end of nothing nibbled to a very fine sliver. With Kyp on my side, there was no contest. You could see they knew it, too. They just sat there, patiently. Waiting for an invitation.

I made the error of meeting their eyes, which they mistook for a gesture of friendship, and the three of them nodded, almost in unison. They didn't exactly ask for some of our scavenge. They didn't even look right at it. One of them began preening. The other two studied the forest floor, looking like getting something to eat was the last thing on their minds. They shared, I thought, a resemblance to one of my more pious great-great-aunts. Straight neck. Straight back. Everything straight. They perched there, with their beaks closed, looking skinny and cold, the wind ruffling their tatty feathers.

After the silence had stretched a little thin, Kyp asked, "What brings you here, Cousins?"

"The Maker," the one on the left responded, and I began to wonder if the others possessed the ability to talk. Then the male on the far right added, not very helpfully, "Kwaku said you would be here."

I shot a look over at Kyp, but he just shrugged. "Kwaku? Who's Kwaku?" I inquired, when it became clear no one was going to explain.

"This one," the female said, nodding to the shortest one, in the middle.

Whatever other abilities the runt she'd pointed out might have had, tidiness wasn't one of them. His crown feathers sprouted in all directions, and the rest of him was desperately in need of a lengthy, diligent preening.

"Kwaku," I persisted, "you *knew* we would be here?"

The one they called Kwaku nodded.

I was about to ask how when the one on the right interrupted with "We're here to join you."

Well, I opened my beak, and then closed it again. I didn't even know where to begin. "Why?" I asked finally.

"Because Kwaku said you would be here," the one on the left answered, carefully articulating each word like I was a little slow-witted.

I exchanged another look with Kyp and tried to communicate as subtly as possible how desperately I wanted to avoid saying anything that even remotely sounded like "We would be pleased to share your company."

"What did you mean," asked Kyp, who must have been feeling equally lost, "when you said Kwaku told you we would be here?"

The female sat a little straighter, as though she knew in advance how silly this would sound. "The Maker," she explained, "whispers in Kwaku's ear. He knows things ahead of time."

Perfect! I thought, starving *and* crazy.

To my very great surprise, and despite my clear expressions of disapproval, Kyp then invited them to share our meal. Fearing that Kyp had mistaken my stunned silence for agreement, I took him aside while the strangers ate.

"*Let* them eat," I hissed, "even though they didn't find the food, or bring the food here, or deal with the owl. *Let* them have it all, if you want. But after they've finished, just tell them Good eating and let's *fly on*."

"What does it matter," Kyp argued, "if they join us? More eyes make a better watch, and maybe they have stories to share. *You* like stories."

I glanced over at them, huddled around the rabbit, eating like they hadn't eaten since food was invented. "Stories?" I snorted. "*Those* three? The only stories they have begin with 'I'm' and end with 'hungry.' *Those* three beggars? Those three" — I searched for the right phrase — "*bug catchers*? What use are they to us?"

"There's nothing wrong with bug catching," Kyp answered mildly. "We all do our share of bug catching. And who says they have to be of use? Maybe, as they said, the Maker sent them."

"The Maker!" I protested. "Kyp, the Maker sends *good* things. The Maker sends sunrises, spring thaws and good eating. The Maker sends blessings, helpful visions and direction when you're lost. The Maker doesn't send three skinny, scraggly, shaggy Crows too weak to fly and too small to fight."

Kyp stared straight at me. "We both know," he said evenly, "that the Maker can be mysterious about what she sends, and how she delivers it."

I blanched, realizing my error. Then I peered back at the strangers. "*Look* at them," I pleaded. "The three of them together don't weigh as much as what I leave behind after I've *finished* a good meal."

"Something's coming," the one they called Kwaku announced.

"Pardon me?" Kyp asked.

"He said, 'Something's coming,'" the female repeated.

"What?" I inquired as patiently as I could.

Kwaku tipped his head as if listening and then said, "I'm not sure. But you won't want to stay here very much longer."

I turned to him. "Are you asking us to abandon our salvage before it's finished?"

"We can take it up into a tree, if you'd like," he replied, "but I wouldn't stay down here with it."

"Why?" I asked.

"Just a," he hesitated, "just a feeling that I'm getting."

"Go on," Kyp said to me. "Let them carry it up. They may as well finish it off, too. We're both full."

So they carried it up into a maple and continued eating there. Kyp and I flew into the branches of a nearby ash. "Fine. Let them carry it up," I repeated bitterly and glared as I watched the trio peck over the bare bones. "*Let* them have some. They'll have *stories* to tell. You'll *enjoy* the company."

Kyp may have chuckled, which would have infuriated me more.

"Enjoy the company," I muttered. "Mites are

company. Do we enjoy *them*? Fleas are company. Do we invite *them* to fly with us?"

Then, directly below us, without warning, a fox glided into the glade, only a few steps from where we had been eating. It licked its lips, and its eyes regretfully took in the blood, bones and fur strewn about on the ground. Slowly its hungry gaze slid up the tree until, at last, it looked straight at me.

Chapter 15

When we took up the next day, Kyf, Kaf and Kwaku accompanied Kyp and me: Kwaku, the youngest; Kaf, the older brother; and Kyf, the oldest — and, I soon learned, more talkative — sister.

We flew into the wind most of the morning. The cold, hard rain it carried was to be our constant companion for some time. I was miserably chilled and miserably hungry and, in general, just plain miserable. Our new guests didn't do anything to raise my spirits.

I'd spent my time alone for so long that I had become spoiled, used to getting my own way, used to making my own decisions, used to thinking my own thoughts. Flying with Kyp had been easy.

In many ways, he was the perfect companion. He didn't demand much of me. He listened when I wanted to talk. He didn't pry. Flying with Kyp held all the benefits of keeping company and none of the drawbacks.

I wanted nothing to do with these new ones, and since I couldn't convince Kyp to reject them outright, I spent most of the morning's flight in a deep, irritable sulk.

I flew ahead for a while, but flying ahead of Kyp required flying faster than he did. Given my dispirited state of mind, that was more work than I was prepared to do. Instead, I dropped back and brooded behind the others.

Eventually Kyf dropped back as well. I sent some of my brooding silence in her direction. Kwaku and Kaf flew next to Kyp, and the three of them appeared to be exchanging stories, which just increased my resentment.

Here I felt I had cultivated Kyp to a place where he had become adequate company for other Crows, and now Kwaku and Kaf were benefiting from *my* hard work. Very unfair.

Kyf cleared her throat. She was looking in my direction.

"What?" I barked sourly.

"Normally," she said between wing strokes, "the middle sixths are when we stop to eat."

"Normally," I told her, "we don't."

She seemed a little alarmed. "Well, imagine that," she said. "When *do* you stop?"

"We don't," I replied curtly. "We fly all day."

"*All* day?"

"All day. Sometimes we don't roost until late in the dark six. Sometimes we carry on way, way into the night." This was a lie. We almost always stopped for a break, and we rarely flew into the night. But I was feeling angry and impatient and thought maybe she and her brothers could be dissuaded from their stubborn determination to travel with us. She didn't leave, however. And soon enough, Kyp pulled into a grove of maples for an early roost, making my previous comments appear ridiculous.

The few leaves remaining on the trees in this copse were a bright scarlet, and the entire forest floor was awash in rolling, shifting layers of brilliant crimson and ocher. The wind snaked in and out through the trunks and stems, making the leaves rattle and hiss, as if the entire forest was trying to tell us something.

And for Kwaku, it apparently did. He suddenly cocked his head to one side, as though listening intently, and murmured, "That's interesting."

"What?" Kyp asked.

Kwaku listened harder. The leaves spun and whirled for a moment, and he was so immersed in the sounds that he almost seemed to forget we were there. Then he turned to Kyp and blinked.

"I saw all of us just now," he said slowly, "caught in a river. The current curled and flowed around us. It was difficult to see exactly where we were, but we were in danger — that much was clear. It was peculiar," he went on, closing his eyes as if to capture the image more clearly, "because although we were swept along by the current, we were also perched together on a branch, in a tree. And the question was, how to get to the surface?" He opened his eyes. "I don't know. To safety, anyway. And then an answer appeared. No, it didn't appear. It was ... sent. When everything seems to swim, there will be two ways we would normally take. One will dash us, and one will drown us. And the only thing to do is to choose the third way." He blinked again and looked directly at Kyp. "I believe *that* was for you," he said, "but I can't really be certain."

An awkward silence followed.

"But what," I asked, finally, wondering if I was always to be the only one who was completely confused, "exactly *was* that?"

"Predictions often appear to Kwaku," Kyf said, ignoring me and addressing Kyp directly, "in the most unexpected places."

"But *what* is he predicting?" I asked, slightly louder. "A wet autumn? High water and heavy rain?"

"His predictions," Kyf declared, refusing to acknowledge my questions, "always come true. Isn't that right, Kaf?" The terse Crow grunted and nodded.

"That's not exactly right." Kwaku attempted to press a feather into place with his beak. It promptly sprang back up. "*Something* always happens. But I don't always understand what I've seen, so it's hard to say if what happens, eventually, is connected. It's like looking through thick fog. If the wind is right, you can just make out what's on the other side. But if the fog is thick and the wind doesn't shift, sometimes all you get is a glimpse. And then ... after that ... it's just more fog," he trailed off.

"And *what*," I asked, "is the use of predictions you can't be certain of?"

"Use? Oh." Kwaku sounded surprised that I would ask such a question. "No use. I'm not saying they're of use. My experience has been quite the opposite. They've often been useless and awkward."

I must have made a noise that expressed my doubts because Kyf moved farther from me and closer to Kyp — which just raised my irritation to a whole new level. It was plain that the three of them considered Kyp's opinion infinitely more valuable than mine.

"The thing is," she said in a slightly apologetic tone, "he never lies. He only says he sees something when he really *does* see something. And it's not like he *tries* to see these . . . visions. He'll be asleep and wake up having seen something. Or we'll be flying, and I'll look over and find him veering off another way, not paying any attention to where he's going. And then he'll tell me what he saw.

"What other *less perceptive* Crows don't comprehend," she said, shooting me a sharp glance, "is that he doesn't necessarily understand what he sees, any more than I do. Or you. But that doesn't mean that something — and sometimes something important — isn't going to happen."

She had spoken *of* me several times without speaking *to* me, a habit I was finding completely galling. "Well," I interrupted a little brusquely, "I suppose the interpretations of this 'prediction' will have to wait while we deal with our more immediate concerns — like what are we going to eat? I haven't seen anything nearby. Kyp, you haven't. Any of you three?" Of course, they hadn't. "No? Then, it seems to me that we should find ourselves a human roost and scout about for a little of their scavenge."

A not-very-covert glance was exchanged among Kyf, Kaf and Kwaku — another habit of theirs that I was certain would come to aggravate me.

Kaf muttered quietly, "You'd better tell him."

Kyf and Kwaku held a private, only partially audible, animated discussion, and finally Kwaku said, "Go ahead."

I had forgotten how traveling in groups could test your patience. "What now?"

"Kwaku," Kyf told me, "has a bad feeling about that."

"About *what?*"

"About going to the humans now."

"Oh, Great Crow in the Nest!" I exploded. "How does he expect us to eat?"

She shrugged. "Kwaku is never wrong."

"Never *wrong?*" I raged. "Never *wrong?*" When I'm upset, I shed feathers. Three were floating to the ground. "And how hard can *that* be, if all he has is a 'bad feeling' about humans? What does *that* mean? A bad feeling about the way humans *sound?* About how they *smell?* Or just a bad feeling about everything human in general?"

"Well," Kwaku answered mildly, clearing his throat, "I don't think I would say it's a bad feeling I have about humans in general. Although, generally speaking, they *are* a pretty bad bunch. And I would suggest that it — whatever it is — has something to do with you. You and humans."

"*Me* and humans." I think I may have rolled my eyes. "In what way?"

"I don't know," Kwaku said simply.

"Perfect," I responded sourly. "And *so* specific," I added under my breath.

"I heard that," Kyf snapped, glaring at me.

Of course, in the end we didn't go looking for a human roost. Instead, we all stalked like overgrown robins through drifts of fallen leaves searching for grubs or cocoons, or the odd bug dim enough to be out this late in the season.

While the other three foraged, I took Kyp aside. "Those," I scolded him, "were the *worst* predictions I have ever heard. They can't even really be called predictions. They were just vague statements."

Kyp toyed absently with an empty chestnut shell. "What about the fox that appeared yesterday?"

I sighed. "If you wait long enough, *something* will show up looking for food. There was blood on the forest floor. It was bound to attract things. At least," I pleaded, "let's not let these 'predictions' control how we live our lives. We haven't had much to eat," I pointed out quite reasonably. "For all his abilities to 'predict' things, Kwaku hasn't foretold where food is to be found. It's warmer near the human roosts, and there's always plenty of good eating."

"And stingers," Kyp added, "and traps. And cats. Let's just wait awhile. There's plenty of food here — it only takes a little more looking." He passed me an old, soggy portion of a chestnut. "See?"

I squinted at him to determine if he was serious, then reluctantly accepted the nut. After several tries, I even managed to swallow it.

chapter 16

The rain, already cold, grew colder. Food became harder to find. The fruit on the branch had been eaten. The seeds had been scattered. Animals had begun to dig in for the winter. At one point as we were roosting, Kyf was gnawing on a thin, half-closed spruce cone, and I thought, *This* is what we have come to. We've become nuthatches.

Kyp accepted the three skinny siblings easily, particularly the solemn, quiet Kaf, of whom Kyp seemed to have a special understanding. Remarkably little conversation passed between them, but the fragments and silences they shared appeared to carry great meaning. Soon Kaf flew alongside Kyp as though they were brothers. And me? For reasons

I couldn't determine, no matter who I spoke to, it was almost always Kyf who answered.

I did my best and tried to be polite. Silence never truly suited me if there was someone around to speak to, and I suppose I was still feeling a little giddy at being able to both fly and chat after such a long period on my own. And, although she often got under my quills, Kyf had the odd interesting story to tell.

One day, after flying through the morning without saying very much, I finally broke down and asked what had happened to her Clan. Surprisingly, for one who had always had something to say, Kyf seemed reluctant to answer. After a little more prodding, she told me that two days into the previous spring Gathering, Kwaku had experienced one of his visions. "Something's coming," he had said — something bad, I suppose — and then he told the Clan that they should abandon their Gathering Tree and relocate. Well, the Clan had just arrived, stories were being told, Crows were making matches. Naturally, nobody welcomed advice of this sort.

Kyf, frustrated at their lack of discernment as regarded her brother's talents, had confronted their Chooser. "Don't you understand?" she had scolded him. "Kwaku can see things coming that others can't, and if he *says* we should go … Well, we should."

The Chooser, it seems, hadn't appreciated her unsolicited advice, nor the sharp tone it was delivered in. He convened the family Elders and they pronounced a Judgment. Kyf and Kwaku were evicted. Kaf, as quiet as ever, had been left out of their pronouncement, but apparently Kaf told them that what went for the right talon went for the left as well, so all three were Evicted for the spring season.

It was only three days after their Eviction that they spied a fat old raccoon waddling along the riverbank with an adult Crow swinging from its mouth. They flew back a little closer to their Gathering Tree to find the remains of forty or so of their Clan scattered about. The rest of the flock had dispersed.

"I suppose," Kyf said, "somewhere between the time we flew off and the time the sickness struck, it must have occurred to someone that Kwaku had told the truth and that we had been Evicted for nothing." The way Kyf told the story, you could see she had never felt so sad about being so right. I began to understand what Kwaku had meant when he characterized his visions as both useless and awkward.

chapter 17

On we flew, the five of us, always east. Slowly I began to think that maybe, as Kyp had suggested, five Crows were better than one for some things. More beaks. More eyes. At least hawks and buzzards seemed to keep their distance.

But, as my grandmother used to say, good eating doesn't necessarily follow every good greeting, and one look at us told how poor we had been at finding scavenge. We looked like a flock of knotty spruce branches that had suddenly sprouted feathers and learned to fly.

"Something's coming," Kwaku observed one night. And the next day a gale blew in. Kyf remarked that this was the season for storms in this region, and sometimes even stronger ones rolled in.

Well, maybe so, but this blow was big enough. The winds flattened the grasses and stripped trees bare. Any berries left hanging disappeared. Same with nuts. Leaves piled in drifts, covering the ground along with any salvage. We drank rain and ate wind.

After a few days, even Kyp seemed to have lost his patience. One day after foraging till late in the fourth sixth and not finding much more than stones and bones, he shook his wings and snapped that if the wind wanted to blow so badly, it might as well carry us some place better. So up we all went. We flew high, high, high until we found a cold, hard stream of air. Then we wrapped our wings around it and rode it fast, south and east. We traveled day and night, stopping only to drink and let our wings rest enough to support us during the flight the next day. Hills and valleys and streams and lakes rushed by, along with the odd human roost and vast tracks of hoary twisted maples, elms, chestnuts and oaks gripping the hard, stony hills with their long, looping roots. Soon we noticed the smell of salt in the air and realized we'd reached the ocean.

Clouds piled up like a sky of raging surf crashing against the horizon's remote outer edges. The wind churned the water to froth. Sea birds of all sorts, gulls and curlews and petrels, spun and screeched.

The rich smell of seaweed and kelp steeped in brine drifted up to us. But still no food. And everyone was soaked through.

Worse. Now that we had arrived at the ocean and as far east as we could reasonably be expected to travel, the question arose — which direction would we choose? Kyp just stared blankly at the gray foam-flecked waves slapping the rocks and said we'd roost for the night. Maybe, he said, he'd have an answer in the morning.

Dead tired, we dragged our ragged bodies into some dense, thorny brush at the base of a stand of trees, just off the beach. There, we preened and tried as best we could to stay out of the wind and relentless rain.

Still, I couldn't sleep. In the middle of the dark six, as the wind was stroking the tops of the trees and calling to the clouds to come and play, I quietly crawled through the brush and fled the roost. I flew back the way we had come.

If we were going to eat, someone was going to have to steal something, and who among us was best equipped? In short order, I arrived at a human roost I had spotted in our earlier flight. It was beside a long, thin piece of land where pumpkins and beans had been raised. I dropped to the ground to see if any old pumpkin shells or forgotten bean pods were lying about.

That's when I found it. It was about half as long as I am, but thick and still pretty fresh. A choice piece of meat, thrown out by the humans, next to a pile of decaying squash. I performed a quick scout, then picked it up and away I flew, laughing to myself through my clenched beak and the dangling prize. If stealing was this easy every time, I thought, there'd be no honor in it at all.

I returned to the roost just as day was dawning and the others were rising. "Good eating," I announced loudly and dropped the scavenge in front of Kyp, although I think I was performing more for the benefit of the new three. None of them said anything. Instead Kyp sniffed the scavenge, prodded it and cocked his head. "Where did you find it?"

"Near a big tree," I told him. Vague, but not a lie. There had been a pine just to the side of the human's roost. He stared at me for a long moment.

"Did you find it near humans?"

"It might have been near some human place or other," I told him, sounding uncomfortably like a guilty newling addressing his elderly great-aunt. "It's hard to find a place that's *not* near humans."

Kyp hopped closer to the scavenge, peered at it once more, then walked around it, muttering for what seemed like forever. "*Where* by the humans?" he asked finally.

"What does it matter?" I replied, put out that my triumphant return was receiving such a measured response. "Were we supposed to starve?"

Kyp just kept circling it and turning his head this way and that, looking underneath and above it. "There's something funny about this," he said at last, after tapping it several times with his right talon. "Maybe we should just wait."

"Wait for *what*?"

"Why don't I try a very small beakful," he offered, "and we'll see what happens?"

I glared at him, and for good measure glared at the other three as well. Then I said, "Well. That's a bit of a problem."

He looked up from the meat. "Why?"

"Because," I told him, "I already ate some."

There was a good deal of exchanging glances followed by a lot of nobody saying anything. Then Kyp asked, "How much?"

"I was hungry."

"How much?"

"Maybe quite a bit," I told him. The other three were just staring at me now, quiet.

"Kata," Kyp asked after a moment, "how are you feeling?"

"Fine," I told him, but just as the words escaped my beak, I realized I didn't feel fine. Not at all. I felt something else. Like something was squeezing me inside. Maybe it was just the shock of feeling that squeezing, but suddenly I felt dizzy as well.

"Although ... something's not completely right in my head or belly," I confessed. "My throat feels a bit funny, too," I added as I began to feel a kind of tickling near the base of my tongue.

"Funny?" Kyp asked. "How?"

"Tight." Then all at once, I was having difficulty breathing. My legs buckled, and I slid over sideways. I could hear my heart beating fast and so loud it was almost drowning out what the others were saying. And they were all saying *something* now, the four of them. Crowding around close, lobbing questions at me that I couldn't quite make out. And then I heard another voice. A different one.

"Scavenge can be a gift. Scavenge can be a meal. Scavenge," this voice said from a branch beyond the clearing, "can also be a test."

There, perched on the limb of a bush, at the very edge of the clearing, was a Crow like no other Crow I'd ever seen. The crest of her head was all black, like ours, as were her sides, but a strip of the purest white ran up from her belly, around her shoulders and neck and along her back. "The question is," she continued, "can you test true?"

chapter 18

"What are you talking about?" Kyp demanded. "And who are you?"

"What does it matter who I am?" she said. I noticed that she had a curiously clipped accent I'd never heard before. "I'm a stranger. What matters is that the scavenge your friend has eaten is poison."

"How do you know?"

"Even if he wasn't lying on the ground, I would know because the humans have left meat like that out recently. Those that eat it, die." She stared at me, and I couldn't determine if it was a sympathetic glance, or if she was picturing me dead and cold. "When I saw your friend flying with it in his mouth, I followed him."

"It's late to tell me that now," I croaked between bills that were tightening with each passing moment. "Why didn't you say something earlier?"

"You had already eaten, hadn't you? And everyone must test true," she countered in that peculiar accent of hers. "In scavenge and in life, all the same."

"This poison," Kyp broke in, "you've seen it work?"

She nodded. "You eat in the first sixth, you die by the fourth. Many, many birds have met their end this way."

By this time I was feeling pretty awful, pretty sorry for myself and not so very friendly toward this new whatever-she-was, but Kyp managed to stay calm.

"Is there any way to save my friend?" he asked, like he was asking for directions.

She hopped closer until she was almost touching me. I was lying on my right side and couldn't even raise my head. Out of the corner of my eye, though, I could see the vivid, white portion of her neck and belly as she leaned in to look at me.

"Maybe," she cautioned, "if you act quickly and test true."

I couldn't raise my eyes to see Kyp, but for the first time I heard anxiety in his voice. "What do you mean?"

"Listen, stranger. It's not for me to tell you. It is dangerous to give knowledge to someone who has not been tested within Family. But the Maker knows, and by the test one is proven. I can say this. This grove holds what you need. Among my folk, three is sacred. You may have the choice of three. The berries of that bush. The bark of this shrub. The nut of that tree. Choose, stranger. There is only time to administer one, and only one can heal your friend." Then her beak snapped shut, and she returned to her perch.

Kyp quickly asked Kyf and Kaf if they knew anything about the nuts and berries of this area. I couldn't hear a response, so I assumed they shook their heads. Kyp asked Kwaku if he had any special knowledge he could share.

"I can see enough to know that she is speaking the truth," he said slowly, "but which to choose — that is hidden from me."

Another very useful prophecy, I thought bitterly, as a spasm wracked my body.

Kyp hopped from one branch to the next, around the grove. Finally he returned to where I lay. In his beak he carried a sprig with four dark purple berries hanging from it.

By this time it was almost more than I was able to do to open my beak. He crushed the berries and shoved them to the back of my throat, then slid his beak under mine and raised my head. I swallowed hard. The pulp and juice ran down, thick, hairy and acrid. I swallowed again. The bitterness didn't disappear, but grew stronger with every passing moment.

Bitter in the beak, biting in the throat, a fire in the stomach. All at once, I was throwing up everything — berries, scavenge, the nuts and seeds of the past day's foraging. There I was, lying in the mud, vomit and leaves, feeling weak as a mealworm. But my throat was less tight. And my heart was beginning to slow.

This new one hopped down from her perch and leaned in close.

"The Maker has guided you," she told Kyp. "Maybe two days, maybe three, this one will be weak, but the poison is gone."

I had some things that I would have liked to share with her about the Maker and Crows who play games with other Crows' lives, but instead I lay there gasping. Kyp just thanked her for her help — as if she had been helpful!

She cocked her head and for the first time took in the other three as well. "How many of you are there?"

"Just us five," Kyp answered.

"Where do you roost?"

"Here, for now," he replied. "We haven't found anything better."

"The human wanders here as well," she said. "You stay here, the human will find you. And one human I have seen," she added, "has no love for anything that flies or crawls. If that one finds you, you die. Come." She flew to the edge of the grove.

"Where?" Kyp asked.

"I have a roost not far from here. Follow closely," she called over her shoulder as she launched from the branch. "This is the storm season. It's wet."

No fooling, I thought to myself as I slowly climbed to my unsteady talons and followed the others into the driving rain.

Chapter 19

We flew along a ragged coastline, in and out of rocky spires projecting like beaks out of the ocean. I fought to keep up, but I was plagued by cramps and felt frail as a broken spider's web. Below, the water rose and crashed, opened its wide, wet mouth and roared. Gulls swooped down to challenge us, but this new one with the white back simply shouted her defiance.

At last she slipped between two towering stone promontories, and a cleft appeared, half hidden in the shadows beneath the lip of an overhang. The roost entrance to what looked at first to be a shallow hollow deepened into something large enough for all of us. It reeked of gull and tern and old, rotting fish, and the surf's crash and churn entered loud and echoed in ghostly whispers to the back. But at least we were out of the rain and wind.

"You are welcome here," she said as she shook herself and folded her wings.

"This is where you make your roost?" Kyp asked, wondering I suppose, like myself, about the overpowering smell of gull.

"Yes."

"Just you, yourself?" I interjected, making sure.

"Yes," she repeated.

"It's nice," I told her, and by nice I meant musty, smelly, damp and scary, but she didn't answer. I wasn't sure if she didn't care for conversation or just found our accent as difficult to follow as we found hers.

"Were there other birds here once?" Kyp asked, though he must have known there had been. The signs were everywhere, and in every breath we took. Again, she just said yes, and when she didn't provide any details, Kyp asked what had happened to them.

She blinked like it was obvious and said, "I drove them out."

That made me sit up. She was either a very able liar, crazed or one of the bravest Crows I'd ever met. Gulls are, of course, no joke. Some breeds have enormous, powerful wings. A single blow from one can crack a bone, and though their talons are webbed and made more for swimming than fighting, their beaks end in a sharp reinforced nub that's perfect for hooking and gutting fish — or troublesome Crows. Driving gulls out of this cavern would have been very difficult, but she said it the way you'd say "I drank water" or "I went to sleep."

The wind had dropped and the waves settled into a regular pattern that sounded like the world breathing — a long, hushed intake and then a rushing, roaring exhale. Kyf and her brothers had nestled in and gone right to sleep in a tangled pile, but through the gloom I saw Kyp sit up with the new one, and I recognized Kyp's sense of duty in all this. I didn't envy him — conversation wasn't his strength and he must have been exhausted as well. Nevertheless I had no intention of assisting him. I settled in the dark, near a crook in the rock wall, dragged a beakful of brittle seaweed over, shook it to remove any sand or mites and arranged it beneath me.

Kyp was perched next to this new one, a few steps from the entrance. She was having difficulty giving Kyp her full attention — she continually turned her head to keep one watchful eye on the entrance. The mark of living alone, I thought. I know that feeling. Then I realized with a start that I *wasn't* like that anymore. I had gradually become accustomed to flying and roosting with others, to taking my watch and being watched for.

"You've lived here how long by yourself?" Kyp asked.

The new one settled to the floor, then shifted so that she could keep her eye on the entrance. "That depends."

"On what?" Kyp replied, the puzzlement clear in his voice.

"On what you mean by yourself."

I could imagine the expression on Kyp's face. How difficult could this question be? "Did you live with someone?" he enquired finally.

"The first year here, I lived groundward," she replied. "With rats."

My feathers rose so quickly they almost lifted me off the floor. Rats are some of the worst for robbing nests and stealing hatchlings. A chill ran through me. Whatever Kyp felt, he responded calmly. "Rats?"

The moon pierced the clouds, and a single shimmering beam penetrated the cave's entrance. I could see this new one's eyes glinting in the light as she gazed steadily back at Kyp. "When first I came here, Crows wouldn't take me. Gulls didn't want me. I was only a yearling. Would I have survived even a short while on my own? I found a hole in the rocks and I nested with the rats."

Kyp paused as he searched for the right words. "Didn't the rats ..."

"Attack me?"

"Well, yes. Rats — at least the rats back where I come from — aren't known for their ... generosity."

For the first time, I heard her laugh. Just a soft, dry chuckle. "Generous? No, no. The rats were never generous. But every day I bring them food. Every day I fly out and find fruit, fish, scavenge. I eat some, place some in a little pile at the entrance for them. A little bit each time. They liked food, soon they liked me. Even looked for me, for my arrival with food. When I moved into a corner of their den, they didn't bother me. I built a nest, just a small one. The smell of the rats all around was ... powerful, but I was safe there. Rats kept away Crows. Rats kept away gulls. Rats kept away everything. I always remember this. The Crows, my own folk, rejected me, but rats gave me shelter. I ate, shared a little each day. Grew. One day, a big storm came and the tide surged. It rose high over the rocks. Big rats swam, small rats drowned. I moved up during the storm and pushed the gulls from the ledge. That's how I ended up here."

Kyp digested that, then asked, "Where are your folk — your Family and Clan?"

"Time is my cousin. Rocks, wind and waves my Flock," she replied, an edge of bitterness in her voice. "I have lived here four full cycles on my own. Before I lived here, I lived a lifetime away. That direction," she said, and nodded at the opening of the cave.

Kyp peered out into the darkness. "Is there an island there?"

"No, no. Across the ocean."

In the dim light, I saw Kyp's head snap about. "How far is that?"

"Too far. Many days. Count your feathers, then double it. Many, many days," she sighed and was silent a long time. When she began again, her voice was so quiet I only just made out what she was saying over the surge and rush of the surf. "My land, my roost, my kind and kin lie across the water. I was a yearling and stayed close to my mother. One morning a storm came. She and I became separated from our flock. A full day passed before we realized just how separated. The storm turned us about, confused us. We were carried out, far over open water. Out of sight or trace of land. We flew. Flew through the darkest darkness. Flew till our wings could no longer hold us. Then — what's the word? When the Maker does the impossible? A miracle?"

Kyp nodded. "That's right."

"Then, a miracle. Lights pierced the blinding rain. Turns out to be one of those floating roosts humans build. Tired and cold, we took shelter on that human roost. We hid ourselves in one of the dark corners the humans couldn't enter. My mother was too sick to fly and had lost many feathers in the storm. I crept out nights, stole from the humans.

Brought back what I found. Fed her. Preened her. Talked to her. Slept close to warm her."

She stopped speaking. The tide's relentless churning filled the roost. I thought she had decided to sleep, then abruptly she began again, in the same even, controlled voice. "Nothing helps. She doesn't recover. Before we see land, the Maker completes her test, takes my mother under her wing. I am alone after that. No flock. No Clan. Just me and humans, out on the water. I don't know where I am. Don't know where I am supposed to go. One day the fog clears. I know I am near land. But a different land. The smells all new. Sounds I never heard before. I left my mother's body lying among the humans' things, flew to this new place."

Perhaps to keep better watch, or perhaps from some restlessness, she stood, paced to the very edge of the roost and looked down at the surf. "I discovered some things are the same here, but many things — most things — are different. I see Crows. But Crows that look like you. All black. I couldn't speak to them. They spoke another tongue. I approached, they chased me. I thought they won't accept me because I don't know their ways. I learned. Tried again. Again, they chased me. Bit me. Forced me down among the rocks. They told me. Never come again."

She picked up a fragment of shell and flung it out the entrance. "I healed. Ate. Tried returning back across the waves, but those waters are wide, and there is no place to roost when your wings tire. The winds are fierce and storms frequent. I nearly died. Finally, I was forced to return. Then I found the rats."

She turned from watching the ocean to Kyp. "What are you when no one wants you? What are you when there is no place for you? I have made a place for myself. Many times I have asked the Maker to take me, but the Maker tests us and she demands that we all fly true."

She raised her wings and stretched them, then drew them back in. "I am called Erkala ru Erkata ru Eru. Now, you know me. Maybe more than you wanted. What about you, Stranger?" She settled onto the rock flooring again. "What stories can you share?"

There was a long silence, and I could see Kyp struggling to find a polite way to refuse. "I'm not really the one to tell a story. My friend — the one you helped, Katakata — has an infinity of stories. Just get him started once he wakes. He'll tell you."

"But now he sleeps," Erkala protested, "and I haven't heard one in a lifetime of days. Not since my mother flew to the Maker."

After thinking a long while, Kyp finally asked, "What kind?"

"Of story?" She drew some seaweed in close and arranged it around her to keep out the cold. "About you."

Kyp preened a moment and then quietly resigned himself to the inevitable. "I am Kyp ru Kurea ru Kinaar," he began. "I was laid in a nest with four other eggs, in our traditional nesting grounds, west of here. A long way west. Where mountains meet the flatlands. I'm told my mother thought she would be overworked feeding five chicks, but I was the only one who hatched that season. The shells of all the other eggs proved too thin. They simply collapsed. Not just in my mother's nest either. Of the batches laid during that nesting, almost half didn't survive to hatching. Anyway, mine was the only one that hatched in our nest, and I hatched too early.

"Because of the thinness of the shell or the earliness of my hatching, I came out with one leg shorter than the other. I couldn't stand when other chicks my age could. I'd fall over. Many in the flock thought I wouldn't survive. Some thought I shouldn't be fed, that it was a waste of food. But my mother fed me, and an Elder in my Clan, Kalum, sat in the nest with me. He fed me as well and kept a top eye out to see that none of the other Crows interfered. I think I sensed early on that there was something unspoken, that other Crows avoided our nest. And I knew — although my mother never said so — that it meant more than it should have to my mother that I fly well. That the others in the Flock see that I could . . . that I was as able as anyone.

"It came time for me to leave the nest, and I'm sure I was as anxious as any chick. I remember the enormous drop from nest to ground seemed impossibly far. I wondered if I could survive that leap. The elder, Kalum, flew to the nest and sat with me. He told me, 'Kyp ru Kurea, you keep moving. If you don't hold still, it won't matter if your two legs aren't the same size.' So I tumbled over the edge of the nest, and I opened my wings, and I completed a clumsy sort of glide to a lower branch. I started flying that day, and when others would have rested, I didn't. I was still flying that night. I've never looked back."

Erkala nodded. "I saw as we traveled here. You fly well."

"I feel most comfortable," Kyp replied, "in the air."

"I know that feeling," she said quietly, and I saw her looking at him steadily. "A place of comfort — when you are different, it's not so easy to find."

"No. It's not."

"Where are you traveling to?" she asked.

"I don't have any destination," he said and shifted uncomfortably. "I'm looking for a … I'm looking for someone."

"Who?"

"A member of my Family. Of the Kinaar. We were hit by the sickness."

"Ahhh. Here too. I've seen the effect of this illness. Many Crows have been collected by the Maker."

"This one, the one I am looking for, got sick but survived. She was gathered up and taken, along with several others, by the human. I believe — my friend Kata spoke with someone who saw her — that she is somewhere out here."

"You've traveled all this way looking for this someone?"

"Yes."

"Where did they say to look?"

"East."

"East?" She blinked. "That's all?"

"Yes," he said, then added, "in a human's roost."

"There's a lot of east, Cousin. A lot of human roosts."

"Yes."

A long, heavy silence followed, and I could imagine Erkala wondering if we were all crazy. Finally, she matter-of-factly said, "Seems a fool's errand."

Kyp stared at her. "It's the only errand I have. I have a promise to keep."

"How long will you carry on?"

Kyp shrugged. "As long as it takes."

After they had sat silent for so long, I thought they had both fallen asleep, and I was half asleep myself when I heard Erkala murmur, "Then you are looking for a very lucky Crow."

chapter 20

The next day I was still sick. Whatever little strength I'd mustered to fly to Erkala's roost had completely disappeared. I lay limp on my rank bed of crusty seaweed and was thankful for it. Kyp, Kyf, Kaf and Kwaku joined Erkala in scouting for food. I slept, long, deep and untroubled by my surroundings, gull-polluted though they were. When I woke, the sun had nearly set. A small pile of crabs, broken clam shells and a couple of tiny fish heads were arranged near where I was lying. I heard Kyp and the others speaking in low tones, but didn't pay any serious attention. I devoured everything that had been placed next to me, pushed the shells aside, let my head slip back onto the cool rock surface and fell asleep once more.

It was three days before Kyp suggested we leave the roost. I knew that my rest was over when Kyf released a musty beakful of kelp above my head, scattering sand and sea salt, then asked if I was ready to fetch my own food yet. Kaf was grooming Kwaku, to no great effect, and Kyp and Erkala were engaged in a conversation about where the human roost might be.

Erkala reached for a mussel from a small mound she had stacked near the entranceway. "This one," she said as she cracked the mussel against the rock wall. "This one you are looking for. You believe she's alive?"

"I don't know for certain," Kyp replied. "I think so."

Erkala sorted through the broken shells and fished out the soft, pulpy flesh. Tossing it high in the air, she opened her beak and swallowed it in one swift motion. "And the human's roost she is in. Do you have any description of it?"

Kyp shook his head. "Just that it was large. The largest he had ever seen."

Erkala grunted and shoved the empty shells over the edge of the entrance. "That's not much."

"It's all I have to go on."

"If she would be anywhere, it would be farther south. As I understand it, the humans in this area roost mostly in smaller flocks. Fly south and you'll find many more." She wiped her beak against the rock, then stretched her neck.

"Well. Thanks," Kyp said.

"You're welcome," Erkala replied as she performed a quick rearrangement of her wing feathers. "And if you have no objection, I'll join you."

Kyp glanced up. "The other day you said this was a fool's errand."

"That was the other day," she replied and turned her attention to her roost's dark, brine-crusted walls. "There's no future here for me. It may be a fool's errand you're flying, but at least it will take me beyond this cliff, these gulls and this coast. And in the end," she said, stretching her wings, "everything we do in life may be a fool's errand."

Chapter 21

I have had some time to think about this and have decided that there are no accidents. What directed us to that barren shelter along the battered coast? What wind guides the seed that sprouts into the tree that provides support for the nest of your birth? Who could comprehend why Kyp selected a berry that saved my life or what guided a scrawny black and white chick across an entire ocean to fly with us? I only knew that we flew from that roost as a band of six, and six is a sacred number. So I understood then, even if the others didn't. I understood that the Maker had gathered us up in her talons, and there would be no turning back until she had released us, or her dream had released her.

What our group lacked in size, we more than made up for in the difficulties we had with one another. Kaf rarely spoke and when he did it was to Kwaku, Kyf and Kyp. Kyf was respectful of Kyp, protective of her brothers, accepted Erkala and barely endured me. Erkala was suspicious of Kwaku, ignored Kaf and disliked Kyf. Nobody cared for me, with the possible exception of Kyp, and apart from Kyp, I didn't really like anyone. But everyone tolerated everyone else when Kyp was around, and I began to understand that it wasn't only a skill in seeing *things* that Kyp possessed, but a skill in seeing *individuals*. He was able to appreciate something in a Crow that — for whatever reason — was invisible to others. And as the days passed, that skill slowly began to shape us. An order, and a grudging kind of respect, developed among us.

We chose to fly back inland aways — to avoid the wind off the ocean that had grown bitterly cold and the harassment of sea birds and to maintain some tree cover.

A wide, slow-flowing river wound its way south and we followed it after our own fashion — criss-crossing the valley, testing air currents and allowing the steadier ones to carry us and ease our journey. We alternated taking lead, and I found myself, almost against my better judgment, relishing being part of a flock again. Kyf, whatever else she did, made up for Kyp's silence and Erkala's moodiness. Erkala remained uniformly testy, but she was a strong flier and the best and most alert scout anyone could ask for. If there was danger of any sort near, she could be relied upon to see it well before anyone else. And she was totally fearless. Kaf was tireless and completely loyal. He didn't have much to add to a conversation, but he never complained either — of extra watches or sharing food. Kwaku, of course, knew things. While no one understood how he received his information, or where it came from, everyone came to trust it and rely upon his foresight.

We were all very much on our guard. Yet it took us by surprise when we turned a corner in the valley and there, rising, falling and swelling like an enormous cloud of giant midges, was something we had not seen for many, many days. A genuine flock of Crows — more than a hundred of them.

We slowed and cautiously approached, but as we drew closer, we sensed that something was odd. None of the things you would normally have expected to happen did. There was no display. The flock didn't move to roost as we approached, and no one confronted us to defend territory. That's when I noticed — they were almost all yearlings.

Of course, it's not uncommon for small groups to band up over winter and separate again come spring. A group of this size though, and all of them young, struck everyone as strange.

Kyp and Erkala followed protocol and flew ahead. Kyf, Kwaku, Kaf and I perched some distance away. Kyp called "Good eating" and waited for their Chooser to fly out. It took a while for a Chooser to approach, and when he did, he appeared confused about what he was to do.

"Good eating," he called at last. "I am Kyrt ru Kenyk ru nothing. Kyrt, the oldest son from the Family of no one. Of my nest family, I am the only remaining. That's true of almost all those you see here with me. Our Clans were swallowed when the sickness came and our Families shattered. By fate or luck we survived. We banded together as we happened to meet. Truthfully, we didn't expect to survive the summer. But here we are, death didn't want us, and now you arrive. You talk different from us, and clearly you *are* different from us. She" — he nodded at Erkala — "is very different. Let me congratulate you on surviving. Isn't that so, everyone?"

He glanced at the Crows behind him, and his ragged companions murmured their good wishes. He turned to face us again. "Where are you from and what brings you here?"

Kyp spoke for all of us when he said, "I fly from some distance west, near the mountains. These friends have joined me and we are traveling through, on our way south."

"To where?" Kyrt asked.

"I'm not sure yet. I'm looking for someone."

"Have you seen many other Crows in your travels?"

"No," Kyp replied, shaking his head. "The disease seems to have flown ahead of us."

The youngster's face fell momentarily, but he brightened again. "Well. I suppose I didn't expect any different. That's been our experience, too — and you're here anyway. Your long journey sounds unusual to me, but we seem to live in unusual times now, don't we? So perhaps it's all perfectly normal. Let me ask you, is there any scavenge where you're going? We're all a bit hungry."

Kyp was a little startled by the question. "I wouldn't know," he answered. "I can't predict what we'll find, really."

"Well," said the youngster after lifting a talon and scratching himself, "Good eating, once again, and our invitation out to you. It would be wonderful if you would roost with us the night. We are all of us leftovers. We don't have much in the way of rules or plans or organization, but at the very least we could exchange stories."

Kyp, after glancing back at us, gave a nod of assent. "We can stay the night. Thanks."

As the youngster returned to his band, my heart sank. I perched on a branch with Kyp and Erkala, and as we watched the youngsters fly recklessly about, for the first time ever, I felt old. I peered over at Erkala, who wore a stony expression. I turned to Kyp. "Why are we still here? *Look* at them. Why would we want to involve ourselves with this confusion? This band doesn't know up from down. That Kyrt was right — I don't know how they've survived this long. Look at the roost they've chosen. It's too small. It's too bare. It's out on its own. It doesn't offer any real shelter, and as they've pointed out, there's no real food nearby. They feed whenever they want, on whatever they can find — which, given the look of their feathers, doesn't seem to be much — and they've posted no watch." I nodded to Erkala. "You must agree with me."

She gave an impatient twitch of her wings. "I agree that they have no manners and no organization."

"So, we should carry on."

"No," she corrected me as she grimly observed three Crows squabbling over the shriveled remains of an ancient and miniscule shrew carcass. "I think in this, Kyp is right. We should stay."

I stared at her with disbelief. "*Why?*"

She shrugged. "They're young. They don't know better. They need advice."

"Yes, well, as Kemu the hero said, Ignorance is only the first disaster. Others will follow as certainly as rain follows clouds."

Kyp nodded slowly. "True, but you know, I've been thinking. This Plague, it's changed things more than we have understood. It's a new world, Kata, and we're going to have to make sense of it. Somehow we're going to have to find a way to survive in it. And to do that, we'll need to form a new flock."

Suddenly a shrill voice interrupted us. "Food! Food! Food!"

Flying toward us was one of the many youngsters, frantic with excitement, shouting as he came.

Everything in the way he flew indicated how agitated he was. I couldn't understand how he had escaped being plucked up by some owl or eagle. "Everyone! The best of luck! Better than the best of luck! Food and lots of it!" he shrieked. "Follow me!"

The flock didn't waste any time. They dropped whatever they were doing immediately and flew up and off before they had the slightest idea which way they were going. A flurry of Crows swirled in the air, calling "Where?" "He said food?" "What kind?" and "He didn't say." After a quick misstart in what apparently was the wrong direction, they were off.

Kyp viewed the total lack of organization with disbelief. "Well," he asked us, "shall we follow?"

I shrugged. "It can't hurt to have a look."

"I suppose," Kyp agreed, "but let's keep our distance."

The band straggled over a hill, back toward the ocean, until they arrived at an opening next to a coastal marsh. The youngster leading didn't circle or perform any exploration, but dropped directly onto the biggest heap of corn I've ever seen. It was just strewn about in a meadow, as though a passing cloud had hailed cobs instead of hail stones. The band didn't hesitate, but fell on that corn and began feeding instantly. I flew over three times, and Erkala performed an even wider loop.

I returned to perch in a large tree that stood just beyond the clearing, on the seaward side of the marsh. Down on the ground, the youngsters crawled like ants over the small mountain of corn, ripping through the husks with startling speed.

I felt hunger trying to get my attention. "Sometimes luck arrives undeserved," I said aloud to no one in particular. "It's a long time since we saw good eating of this size. And corn! That's fortunate."

Kyp had perched just above me. "But what's it doing there?"

"Well, it's obvious humans brought it here. Why? That's hard to say. Humans often discard food or put it aside. Sometimes they return to it, but other times … it just sits there, and the Crow who finds it quickest is the well-fed Crow."

Erkala sat apart, scorn radiating off her. She shook her head. "The human is ugly, but it's not stupid. Even when we don't understand it, it *never* does anything without a reason. This band" — and here she made a dismissive nod — "has no more idea why the human left its food than why they survive the summer.

There's a human path" — and she gestured with her beak — "just past the rise there. And look, marks on the ground show that one of their moving boxes was here recently. It pushed right through the reeds and the bog. That seems like a lot of trouble for the human to take, without some reason."

I raised my wings and dropped them. "Fair enough — but why?"

No one had an answer.

I glanced over at Kyf for support. She had been saying how hungry she was before we encountered the new ones. "Well," I began again, "obviously we would set up a watch. This bunch don't know what they're doing, that's clear, but we would rotate so someone would be up here to keep an eye out while the rest of us ate."

Erkala didn't say any more, but everything about her body stated how unhappy she was with the notion. Kyp turned to Kyf and her two brothers.

"Kwaku," he asked, "do you sense anything about the corn?"

Kwaku hesitated. "No," he replied finally. "Something's coming. Something." And again he paused as though he was searching far away. Then he shrugged, as the answer eluded him. "But the corn is fine to eat. At least," he added, "there's nothing telling me that it isn't."

"Kyf?"

"Well. For once I agree with *him*," she said, nodding reluctantly at me. "We all have to eat and there's food right down there. I'm starving, and it seems silly not to eat it, and since my brother doesn't have any problems with it, well, I think we should go down."

Kyp turned to me. I shook my head. "I've been wrong before — and not that long ago. If you say we shouldn't eat, I won't — but we're not going to get another opportunity like this soon. And you know and I know that any good eating of this size before first snow is welcome. Kyf, Kaf and Kwaku have been flying on nothing since we met them. Erkala is strong, but there'll be plenty of days in winter when we are flying on the memory of meals we had in the fall. We fill up here, now — and that could make a big difference when it grows colder."

Kyp looked down at the Crows feeding and said, "Let's not rush anything. We can wait a few more moments."

So we waited. And watched those others eat and enjoy it thoroughly while I sat and listened to my stomach protest and complain.

After what seemed an eternity, Kyp flew down and sampled a very tiny amount of corn. He returned to our perch and we waited an even longer period. My stomach rumblings would have done credit to a small but very active thunderstorm. I knew that there was more corn than the youngsters could possibly eat in one sitting, but part of me grew anxious as I watched them gorge.

"How did it taste?" I casually enquired of Kyp.

"Very good," Kyp replied. "There may be something wrong with it, but I'm not the one to tell you from the sample I had." I heard Kyp's stomach growl and realized that he must have been feeling every bit as hungry as I was.

Finally, after I had begun to believe that I might lose my mind if I sat and watched another Crow eat happily for even a single moment more, Kyp said, "If anyone can see any reason why we shouldn't eat, tell me. This band hasn't done any real scouting, but I can't see any danger. After sampling the corn, I still feel fine. And obviously, *they* look happy."

"I'm against it," Erkala said, shaking her head. "Poisons can take effect much later. And it's completely out in the open. At least let us wait until nightfall."

The youngsters continued to pile into the corn and would only occasionally emerge to call to us from time to time. "Come down!" they'd shout cheerily. "The corn is wonderful! There's plenty. Come join us." We just nodded at them sagely and continued to sit silently. I comforted myself by repeating that we were doing the wiser thing. That grew old quickly. The sun edged slowly toward the horizon. I could actually *feel* my stomach writhing and shrinking inside me.

At last the sun slipped behind the trees. I broke the silence. "Well. I think we've done the responsible thing. We've given the food plenty of time." I glanced down at the young Crows, many of whom were now so full they had retired to bushes with a morsel in their talon to pick away at. "And we're all hungry. None of these youngsters shows the slightest sign of getting sick, except perhaps from overeating. Who hasn't seen the human throw things away for no good reason? How is this different from all those other times?"

"Well then?" Kyp asked. No one said anything. Finally Kyp nodded. "Let's eat. I'll take first watch."

I dropped to the ground. The rich, sweet aroma of corn was thick in the air. I plucked up a cob, and the smell was so overpowering and my hunger so great, I almost passed out. I stripped the cob of its husk and began to eat. It was, in every way, the finest corn I have ever, ever tasted: sweet, juicy and crisp. It may have been hunger speaking, but it was good eating of an order I had trouble recalling. Kyf, Kaf and Kwaku went after the corn with a quiet intensity that made you believe they had not eaten since their feathers came in. For the longest time all I heard on the ground was the clacking of beaks and the resonant crunch of kernels. Erkala ate briefly, then insisted on replacing Kyp on watch.

chapter 22

The mood in the roost was festive that night.

The branches of the tree we'd selected seemed to hold some special charm that embraced all of us. Kyp relaxed as it became clear that we could expect no ill effects from the corn. Crowded together near the trunk, the rich smell of pine everywhere, everyone experienced fond memories of when we had all been part of much larger groups. The yearlings, now that they were well fed, seemed especially appreciative of our visit. I think they, having had a pretty hard time of it, took the discovery of the food and our appearance as especially good omens. They gathered in tight knots around each of us, asking for information. Even Kaf, normally as talkative as tree bark, was soon laughing and chatting. Only Erkala sat apart, grimly folding her wings and requesting an extra watch. She called Kwaku over and the two of them talked quietly for a short time before he returned and sat, as usual, with Kyf and Kaf.

Is there anything quite like the feeling of having a really full belly as darkness drops? We all found our places in the tree and got comfortable in the branches' welcoming hollows and dips. I couldn't have asked for a more attentive audience — there were tales these yearlings had never heard. The stars emerged overhead, clear and vivid from horizon to horizon — what my mother referred to when I was a chick as the "night flock come to roost."

A fine, shimmering hint of mist hovered at the edge of the sky, promising a thick fog by morning. We laughed and talked until our throats were raw. Erkala, who had taken watch for so long, at last concluded that nothing associated with the corn presented any danger and — having posted two yearlings to spell each other off — fell asleep. Eventually the water slapped and lapped and lulled even the most wakeful, exuberant partier into a deep, contented slumber.

chapter 23

Click.

Kyp opened his eyes. It was late in the dark sixth, and he was drenched with dew. As expected, a thick, heavy fog had rolled in and now swirled about us like a hazy river of eddies and currents. Mist filtered through the branches and coiled about the leaves. One moment, there was Kwaku, nestled in the crook of a branch; the next moment, the mist erased him as though he had never existed.

Kyp cast his eyes about, searching for the sentries that Erkala had posted, and found them fast asleep, their heads tucked under their wings. He cocked his head to one side. There are different kinds of silence. Silence can be peaceful — the unthinking, careless silence of sleep. Silence can be joyful — the silence of achievement. Silence can be tense — the silence of waiting and watching. Now, Kyp waited.

The mist billowed and curled. In that moment, the evening in the tree took on the shapeless quality of a dream. Kyp squinted through the fog-dimmed moonlight and wondered whose dream it was.

Then the mist parted and Kyp spied something far down on the landward side among the taller grasses. The mist shifted again, and the image disappeared. Kyp froze. The image he had half seen was of a human draped in a kind of skin that resembled the reeds and grass. Kyp peered through the billowing mist and glimpsed the head of another human farther back, nestled in among the rushes. Clutched in the arms of this human was a long, black, glittering stick. The human slipped something into it.

Click. The curious snapping noise broke the silence again.

Dreams can be nightmares too. In that moment, everything took on the eerie quality of a terrible, relentless dream as things moved painfully slowly. To Kyp, on his perch, surrounded by sleeping Crows, there suddenly seemed no possibility of escape. If he raised the alarm and the flock lifted, the motion would surely alert the humans and their stingers would make short work of them. If they didn't fly, eventually the mist would burn off, and they would be exposed.

Staying close to the trunk, using the cover of the leaves and fog, Kyp silently slipped next to me.

"Wake up," he whispered.

"What?" I raised my head, opened eyes still heavy with sleep. I saw Kyp staring at me through the fog, like a ghost.

"Shh," he said, barely moving his beak. "Don't talk. We're surrounded by humans —"

"Humans!" I tried to shake off my fatigue.

"Shh! Don't talk, just wait." He immediately turned to Kwaku, who was sleeping a branch up from me.

"Kwaku!" he hissed. Kwaku blinked and woke. "I need you to tell me. Is this the place you saw in your dream?"

Kwaku blinked once more and glanced about. "It looks very much like it."

"Did the dream tell you what I was to do?"

Kwaku turned and looked at him. "You *know* what to do. The third way."

"I don't know any 'third way,'" Kyp whispered and then stopped and looked down near the talon end of the tree, where the marsh waters lapped. "Unless."

"Unless what?" I asked.

"We can't fly, and we can't stay," he muttered, and paused again, lost in thought. Finally he looked up. "Don't use your wings, and don't call out. The moment the humans see or hear us stir, we're finished. That's why the corn was scattered, to draw us all to this place where they can arrange themselves around us and kill us. We have to wake everyone, but quietly. Can you do that?"

I nodded. "And then what?"

"Then everyone has to climb down the tree."

"*Down?*"

"Yes. Talon over talon — no flying. Stay as much as possible on the water side of the tree. Make sure everyone understands. Absolute silence. Once they get to the ground, then and only then can they fly. But not up! When they fly, it has to be at the same level as the water, through the channels in the reeds. Not one feather can be seen over top of the reeds — that's important. Do you understand?"

I nodded again.

"We'll meet on the far end of the bay, in the inlet shaped like a wing. Do you remember the one I'm talking about?"

"We flew over it yesterday."

"That's right."

Silently, so silently even the tangled mosses that dangled from the twigs didn't stir, we pulled ourselves along the branches. We found one Crow, told him. He told the next, and so on. Beak to beak. Then each one started its own silent descent. We all remained pressed close to the trunk to keep the tree between ourselves and the humans — even so, every moment we expected to hear explosions and feel fire.

The mist was already beginning to thin, taking on a pearly sheen as the day grew closer to dawn. As soon as the sun slipped over the horizon, the sheltering mist would disappear.

Kyp remained in the tree, delivering a quiet word and direction where he could. Finally, when there were only a few talonsful of youngsters left and myself, I gestured for Kyp to go. He gestured back that he would wait till the last had left.

The final two Crows to go — Kanyt and Kymyt, the sentries who had fallen asleep — had just landed groundward, and I was following. Kyp was behind, about halfway down the tree, when all at once a weight dropped on his back and a searing pain tore through the base of his neck. He crumpled, stumbled and fell to his side on a broader branch just below. The fall dislodged the weight and freed him of the paralyzing pain. He quickly shook his head and rose to his talons. There, turning and regaining its feet, was the cause. Lithe and sinewy, its thick brown and black pelt gleaming, legs churning to reestablish a firm grip against the bark, mouth agape and bristling with teeth, the weasel scrambled back along the branch toward Kyp and sprang.

As the body hurtled at Kyp, he had to choose between the weasel's jaws and the humans' stingers.

But as he threw himself from the branch and felt teeth latch on to his left shoulder, he realized that he had waited too long.

Plummeting, Kyp twisted, trying to find a hold on the weasel's body for his talons. The fog had thinned sufficiently that the disturbance created by the two grappling bodies swept an opening in the mist. Instantly, fire, smoke and a deafening blast erupted from the humans. Pieces of twigs, bark and leaf were shredded and scattered, branches snapped, spinning through the air. The weasel, struck on its hind quarters, was cut in half, its head and shoulders severed and sent flipping over Kyp. The force of the explosion spun Kyp around and hurled him through the leaves and twigs of an adjoining branch. The two fleeing youngsters, Kanyt and Kymyt, terrified by the noise and sudden blinding light, tried to escape by flying up.

"No, *down*! Stay down!" Kyp cried, but even as he was shouting, the youngsters emerged over the tops of the reeds, their flailing wings pushing aside the sheltering fog. The stingers opened up again, and the two were cut to pieces mid-flight, their feathers ripped from their bodies and scattered over the water.

chapter 24

We reconnected along the shores of the inlet as Kyp had planned, then fled almost at once when Kaf spotted humans moving across the water on floating boxes. We flew south and inland until at last a quiet glade in a wooded valley opened up beneath us.

Kyp selected a dense grove of chestnut trees that provided protected access to water. Long sloping limbs dipped low over a river, and a thick, concealing mat of gooseberry bushes sprang up beneath. Kyp gave the call and we dropped. The band organized themselves along the branches and we settled to preen and clean.

The grove was situated in the middle of a narrow valley split into halves by a long, thin, twisting human track. The track wound along beside the river, spanned the water and then disappeared into a dark cave farther up the valley. The air in this glade was still and refreshingly quiet.

Kyp grimaced as he set about rearranging his feathers. Erkala landed beside him and watched. "Is there much pain?" she asked awkwardly.

"Some," Kyp replied, "although I suppose I should count myself lucky for what the weasel did to me, when I consider what the humans did to the weasel."

Erkala shook her head. "I have to apologize."

"For what?" Kyp asked. "You were right."

"No. I was wrong," she objected, her voice expressionless. "I thought that by posting two of the yearlings to keep watch, one at least would stay awake. I should have known. They had no practice and no understanding of the importance."

"You'd warned us," Kyp objected again. "You are least of all to blame." But Erkala just shook her head, closed her beak and withdrew to a branch apart from the rest of us.

Kyrt, having overheard the conversation, flew up beside Kyp. "I'm sorry for Kanyt and Kymyt — they were two brothers who joined us late in the season — but if we had flown from the tree, as we normally would have" — he shook his head — "we would have been destroyed. All of us." He glanced around at the other yearlings perched in the tree.

"We're grateful to you."

Kyp stretched his sore left shoulder, trying to work some of the pain out of it. "I was somehow awakened by the humans' preparations. It was just good luck."

"Maybe. But good luck is rare for us this season, and there's not a one in our band who doesn't feel thankful to still have their feathers."

"Well. You're welcome," Kyp yielded and continued his preening.

"And," Kyrt continued, "if it's all right, we'd like to fly together a while longer."

Kyp met Kyrt's eyes. "You understand what I've told you?" he asked. "That I have no set destination? No roost or refuge? That I'm searching for someone?"

"Yes. I understand. And we — all of us — will help you however we can."

Kyp briefly outlined his plan, such as it was. It was, I think, a sign of just how inexperienced Kyrt was that he saw nothing odd in our quest. He simply listened and, when Kyp was finished, shrugged and said, "South it is. And if you are looking for one of the larger human roosts, there's one that's not that far."

Kyp squinted at him. "What do you mean?"

"A relative from a Clan farther south attended our Gathering half a cycle back. He said Crows that range the coast just south of his territory talk of a human roost that they call 'The Maker.' They said it was the largest human roost they'd ever seen."

At that moment Kyf flew down and interrupted. "There's clean water, right there, and you're still talking," she scolded, practical as always. "*You* should get down there and wash yourself of all that blood and weasel smell before something ugly comes looking."

Kyp and I left Kyrt to consult with the rest of his yearlings and dropped to the riverbank. Kyf flew alongside, clearly looking for an opportunity to say something else to Kyp. "My brother has shared something with me, and I can't stop worrying about it," she said in a hushed voice. "I think you should speak to him."

Kyp looked concerned. "Did Kwaku receive a warning?"

She shook her head. "No. It's Kaf I'm talking about."

She caught Kaf's eye, and the solid, quiet bird separated himself from the perch and reluctantly fluttered down by the water.

Kyp turned to him. "What is it?"

Kaf coughed and adjusted his feathers. "The thing is," he began finally, "I've been thinking."

Kyp waited patiently for him to continue.

"It's just — the humans and their stingers," he blurted. "Why would they do that?"

Then he peered at us, expectantly, as though this question had somehow clarified things.

"Well," I answered, a little impatiently, "who knows? Who can understand the human." I had spent more time around the human than any of them, of that I was pretty sure — and what seemed a puzzle to Kaf appeared completely obvious to me. "The human can't stand Crows because we steal from them. That's something we know from First Times. They're selfish, unpredictable and savage."

"Yes, but." Kaf glanced awkwardly at us. "That group, the yearlings. They were starved. If they were stealing from the human, they hadn't been very successful. Right?"

"Yes," Kyp agreed.

Those youngsters knew nothing about theft — that much was obvious — but I still couldn't see where this was leading.

I believe Kaf was waiting for us to understand the implications of what he was telling us. When we didn't, he continued in his halting fashion. "Well. The human set that corn out to draw in Crows, don't you think? I mean that *must* be why they did it. And it was quite a bit of work for them, wasn't it? And organization. And it was unusual, too. I mean, I've never seen humans exert themselves that hard to kill us."

Again, Kyp nodded. "I've heard of such things happening from other Crows, but I've never experienced anything like it. That's true."

I still wasn't following him. "So? What's your point?" I asked bluntly.

"So, this must have been done to kill Crows who have been troubling them. *We* haven't been stealing food. The *yearlings* obviously hadn't." He glanced about at us. "So, who did the humans set that trap for?"

Suddenly the valley exploded with sound. Shaken and nervous as we all were, the entire band rose from the riverbanks and the limbs of trees in alarm. Bursting into view along the narrow human track, moving boxes emerged at the northern end of the valley, roaring and wheezing, each black box clinging firmly to the one in front and in turn being clung to by the one behind.

The monstrous thing rattled past for the longest time, and I marveled again at the infinite ways humans have discovered to generate bowel-loosening, gut-wrenching, soul-destroying noises. This ... thing stormed through the valley, annihilated every other sound, and as if its rattling wasn't enough, at the valley's southern end, it released a long, shrill, trailing whoop that ricocheted back and forth among the hills.

At last, it slid into the tunnel, each segment nattering after the first in a diminishing rattle, rattle, rattle. Then it was gone.

The valley grew still again, and we settled wearily

into the trees. Unlike the previous night, there were no jokes or laughter. A few Crows shared muted conversations, but the anxiety caused by our encounter with humans had sapped the spirit of every Crow in our band. Trying to calm everyone, Kyp turned to me and, for the first time that I could remember, requested a story.

I had been shaken so badly, though, that I wouldn't have been able to deal honestly with the most sacred tales, nor do any justice to the funnier ones. Kwaku, his feathers in an even more than usual state of disarray, was attempting without success to massage them into order. I reflected that he could work at those feathers from sunrise to sunset and still end up looking like the last tumbleweed of summer. "I've never heard a story from you," I pointed out. "Why don't you share one with us?"

He patiently pressed one last tail feather into place, then watched as it twisted and bounced back up. "I don't have the command of stories you have," he said and valiantly went back to preening that tail feather.

But the youngsters must have been story starved, and they pleaded so energetically that at last he yielded.

"I've heard Kata tell the story of Sun Eagle to some of you," he began quietly, "and this story has been repeated many times in my Clan as well, but some of the oldest Elders say there's a part of the story that follows. Maybe some of you know it. Maybe it is new to you. My mind has certainly been returning to it lately."

He adjusted himself on his perch and glanced down at the gray-green river flowing beneath the branch. "It's said that following the return of Sun Eagle, the creatures of the Earth listened to the Maker for a long time, but as my father often said, the fox always returns to the bone. Eventually, everybody returned to their old ways and started complaining again. Owl said, 'Why should I hunt at night?' Raccoon said, 'Why should I stay near streams?' Everybody began taking this and doing that. No peace, no order.

"The Maker traveled quietly from place to place and saw that they had completely forgotten her. She warned the creatures, 'Live like you should,' but nobody listened. Everybody was too busy.

"The Maker grew impatient. Slowly, her heart hardened, and she said, 'Better let it rain.'

"Sky darkened. Clouds gathered. Water started coming down.

"At first everyone just squinted up and said, 'That's good. I like the rain.'

"Two moons later, though, it's still raining, and they're hunching their shoulders, tucking their head under a sheltering wing, saying, 'That's enough.'

"Four moons later, rivers flood their banks. Mudslides race down hillsides. Trees are washed away. Where to go? No one knows. Now, there's no place to roost. No good things to eat. Now, everyone's saying, 'This is too much.'

"Maker nods, says to herself, 'Better let it rain some more.'

"Down it comes. Rain like a river pouring over the edges of the sky. Rain like it will never stop. Pretty soon, there's nothing but water all around. Maker looks about and says, 'That's good.'

"She glides over the world to see what she's done. What a view! Bushes all gone. Trees all gone. All under water. Even the mountains. Water everywhere. She nods and finally the rain stops. Sun Eagle emerges, and the light glitters and ripples and shimmers on the surface. Everything's quiet except for water lapping.

"The Maker listens to the silence. Maybe she's a little sad. Then she looks closer.

"There — way down in the water — there's the human. Soaked to the skin. Hair matted. But it's paddling about, tying together some reeds that have floated up and making a shabby floating roost for its folk. And it's bending over and scooping up some of those thinner grasses that have risen to the surface and it's slipping them in-and-out-in-

and-out-in-and-out and it's making a web, and it's catching things with it. And the things it's catching, it's looking at and some of them it's throwing back, but some of them it's eating.

"The Maker glanced a little to her left. Down in another part of the water is Otter, and what's he doing? He's swimming and he's pulling up stalks of kelp, and he's floating on his back. And every so often he's diving down, down, down to the murky, muddy bottom and when he reemerges, snorting and snuffling, he's got a shell in his paws. He's cracking it on his belly and eating.

"And Great Crow? He's skipping from one piece of driftwood to another. Stopping awhile and resting, shaking the water from his wings and cursing, then hopping to another piece of wood. And every time the human looks away, he's stealing some food from it and —"

Suddenly Kwaku stopped, tipped his head to one side, as though listening, then craned his head west. "Something's coming," he said slowly.

I'd grown to hate hearing him say that.

Moments later, Kyf said, "I hear something now. Can any of you hear it?"

Abruptly, the wind lifted from the northwest. Only the wind, I thought. But sure enough, a short time later, one of the scouts Kyp had set at the valley's rim, flew back to us, calling the alarm. Even as she flew toward us, the sky in the northwest grew dark. Clouds gathering, I thought.

But they weren't.

I'm not sure what struck me first, the sound or sight. Maybe it was the combination that suddenly made things clear. What I saw wasn't clouds, and the sound wasn't wind — it was the growing, insistent clamor of a huge flock of Crows flying our way.

The flock swept forward, cresting over the horizon on the north and west — a flock much larger than any of us had ever seen. Sixty or seventy thousand birds rode the wind. The western sun was eclipsed by Crow bodies and wings. The flock pressed on and settled, as ash settles from an immense fire, upon the trees behind and in front of us.

Kyp watched as the landscape turned dark with Crows, then said, "Kuper."

chapter 25

Erkala's head snapped as she turned to Kyp. "You know these Crows?"

Kyp squinted up at the sky. "One of them."

Then this big Crow, maybe three times my size, separated from the flock, fluttered to the topmost branch of a tree directly next to ours and said, "It *is* you."

No one missed the frost under that greeting.

"Good eating," Kyp replied tightly.

The big one flew closer and settled in a branch of the tree we were perched in. He peered so long and so intently at Kyp that a rumble of unease began among his own enormous flock. "How is it possible?" he asked at last.

Kyp returned the stare. "I didn't drown."

The dislike that simmered between these two was lost on no one. "No," the big fellow said after a moment, "it seems you didn't." Then he regained his composure. "Do you Choose for these ones?"

Kyp shook his head. "We fly together. That's all." At the time, I found his tone so casual I felt slightly insulted. It was only later that I realized he was trying to separate us from him for our safety.

The big one stretched his head to one side, as though trying to work out a knot of tension. "What brings you so far from the roost?"

"You know. I've told you," Kyp replied. When this new one, this Kuper, just stared blankly, Kyp said, "Kym."

Something in that name seemed to upset Kuper and he peered hard at us. "Is she with you?"

"No. I'm going to find her."

The big one squinted at Kyp and tilted his head. "Where?"

"In the human's roost." Kyp nodded down the valley. "South."

When he realized this was the extent of Kyp's information, Kuper threw back his head and laughed. "Is that all? Cousin, if that's all you have to go on, I can see why it's taken you so long. I can't believe you're still looking for her."

Kyp's eyes burned, but his voice remained calm. "I can't believe you're not."

Kuper straightened at the slight. "There are more important things to be done," he countered stiffly. "And now I must speak with these others in your band."

"Feel free."

Kuper flew to the crown of the tallest tree, glanced about the valley. "Cousins!" he called at last. "Cousins. What strange times these are. Plague and poor weather. Meager feed. Water poisoned. Forests leveled. Nesting grounds destroyed or fouled and built upon."

He turned his head and took all of us under his gaze. "The Maker is speaking to us, Cousins, have no doubt, the Maker is speaking to us. We retreat to the forests. We retreat to the mountains. To the coast, where we compete with gulls and terns and scuttling crabs for whatever charity the tide might deposit. To the marshes, where we sift through the mud alongside your storks and cranes. We pray and we purify — and what good does any of it do us?"

He stopped and looked at us intently. "Is there anyone here," he called suddenly, "so naive that they believe this Plague doesn't taste something of human?" Then his voice lowered and became thick with contempt. "Cousins, what has *happened* to us?

The Maker is speaking to us, and what is she saying? She is asking if we have *forgotten* who we are. She is *reminding* us that we were here before the rest of the world was hatched. That we were created before the rest of creation. She is *telling* us there is *no point* in flying anymore."

The flock in the trees around us rumbled their agreement. Kuper shouted, to them as much as to us, "Tell me. Can we outfly the Plague?"

His flock thundered back their response, "*No*!"

He nodded. "No. It clings to us the way tree rot clings to an ailing tree. The Maker is telling us, my brothers and sisters, as clearly as if she were perched on this tree with us. If humans have food, she says, take it. If humans level the trees of our nests and then plant trees in their own colonies, she says roost where the trees grow. She says stop purifying. Why should *we* purify when it is the human who is unclean? Cousins, what is this Plague but the Maker warning us? She is saying, 'Change! The old ways will no longer do.' She says, 'Collect yourself and prepare!'"

The response of his flock was so enthusiastic that we could no longer hear him. He waited until they were silent.

"We," he called, glancing back at his flock, "are [illegible] Collection. Brothers, Sisters, listen. The Maker [illegible]mands nothing from us except obedience. The

Maker says fly together, and we do. She says take what you need, and we take it. She says bring my message to others, and we bring it. Join us now, and what will you receive? Good eating and a Family who can defend you. The Collection is rough. We have traveled hard, from the west and south, gathered remnants of flocks who fled, confused and shaken from their territory. But we have farther to go yet, and more Family to collect. Join us and you join a new roost, a new way of living, and a Family that flies unafraid. Choose."

With that, Kuper closed his beak and returned to Kyp's perch. "How will you fly?"

"I speak only for myself. I have a promise I made and I cannot break it."

"And what about the others?" Kuper asked.

"We'll hold Forum, and I'll discuss your offer with them."

Kyp turned to go. "But when you do," Kuper said, stopping him, "tell them there is a matter of territory."

Kyp nodded slowly and flew back to us.

Kyf was the first to greet him. "Good. You're back," she snapped. "Now that this loud talking one has shut his beak, let's move along. Join them! I would no more join them than I would a flock of vultures. I don't need the likes of *him* telling me what the Maker wants or doesn't want, and I don't need *him* to instruct me about how to obey the

Maker. Who does he think he is? He's worse than the Chooser of my old flock."

"Wait," Kwaku interrupted. "What did he say to you — just before you left?"

"He told me to tell you all there is a matter of territory."

A groan ran through our band.

"I should have expected it would come to this," I said. "Whose territory are we perched in?"

"This is Korm territory," Kyrt answered. "Their Clan was closely related to the fifth part of our greater Family. We even had some of the Korm in our band a few moons back, but they died. The rest are Plague scattered." He squinted at Kuper's flock. "There are probably some Korm in there. I think I've seen a few — maybe ten, I doubt more — but enough that he can make a claim."

Kyf shook her head. "He's declared territory? Well, it's plain that if we don't accept their invitation, he means to fight us. What choice is there? All we can do is appear to join now and separate out on our own later."

"He'll have thought of that and will be watching us. I say we fly anyway," Kyrt disagreed.

"We won't get through them," Kaf objected, "and even if we did, they'd catch us eventually."

Kyp interrupted. "There's another option." We looked at him. "We can settle this by Challenge."

"Challenge? I haven't heard things settled by Challenge since I was a newling. I assume it would be you who would take the Challenge?" Kwaku asked. Kyp nodded. "I don't mean to be rude, and I don't want to offend you. But we have to speak honestly, and I don't know that you could win."

"Would the loud talker even accept?" Kyf asked. "He doesn't have to. He already has the advantage of numbers."

"I don't know," I said, shaking my head. "But I think that's what he wants. His quills have been on end since he arrived."

"I agree," Erkala mused and glanced back at Kuper. "What have you done to put a mite under this one's feathers? But Kwaku is right as well. You fight this one, and at very best all I see is you end up with something broken. What is he? Part Raven?"

"No, he's Crow," Kyp answered. "For a time he flew with the Kinaar."

"Well," Erkala continued, "the size difference is too much. When you draw in close to use your talons, the advantage will be all to him. Have you fought him before?"

"Yes."

"And?"

"He snapped my wing."

Erkala shrugged. "That settles it then. I say we *all* fight."

Kyf gestured to the branches across the valley swarming with the newcomers' bodies. "There are thousands of them."

Erkala shrugged again. "The Maker sets us tests. Some we lose." Then she shot a dark look at Kuper. "But if we lose, that big one there comes to the Maker with me to explain."

Whatever else, I thought, it is good to have Erkala on your side.

The wind had continued to grow. Geese could be heard honking to one another, and far off in the south one could hear the faint rumbling of the human's moving boxes. Suddenly Kyp stretched his wings. "We're not going to do either of those things," he announced. "Someone I knew once said, 'Never fight an eagle like an eagle, and never let an opponent choose the battle.' Listen to me, all of you, because I have to talk fast."

chapter 26

Kyp left us and circled slowly to the center of the clearing, where Kuper rose to greet him.

"Good eating, Kurea."

"Kuper —" Kyp began.

The big Crow interrupted him. "Kuper was my name. No more. Since then I have been given a new one, from the old tongue: Urku. It means 'the Collector.'"

"I prefer your old name, if that's all right. And if it's not, well, that's too bad. I'm not about to memorize any of your new names. In any case, my band has declared."

"And?"

"They've declared to settle by Challenge."

Kuper remained impassive. "A mistake," he said. "I assume they wish you to act as Chooser. And they will stake the decision on the outcome of this Challenge?"

Kyp nodded.

"All to the good. We can finally finish what was interrupted. Have your folk retire beyond the clearing."

Kyp returned to our tree, spoke briefly with Erkala. She led our band to a grove of trees on the edge of the clearing. Kyp joined Kuper high above the river.

"According to custom," Kuper called, "Challenge between Choosers can decide matters of Flock. The way of Challenge is clear. Who wins the Challenge, wins Choice." He turned his attention to Kyp. "Let's begin."

The wind picked up and winter's first gossamer snow began to filter down.

Kuper wasted no time and flung himself at Kyp, trying to close and grapple with him. Kyp dropped beneath that first strike and arced back above. Kuper, with his longer wings, sought to catch and close with Kyp, but Kyp's reaction time was quicker, and each attack that Kuper made somehow went wide. When he did manage to close, he used his weight and the two sank in the air. Kyp always twisted away before any real damage was done, but if nothing else, Kuper must have been tiring him.

Slowly the fight climbed higher and higher. We Crows generally fly at the level of treetops, or just slightly above, but eagles and hawks prefer the upper reaches, and they could certainly cut out one of the two and fly off with them, so both Kyp and Kuper had to keep their top eye open even as they fought.

Kuper struck again and missed. Kyp rose higher.

At a certain height, flight itself becomes a trial. The air grows thinner and each breath leaves you short of the air you need.

"Fight!" Kuper gasped as he struggled after Kyp. "Fight! Is this how you Choose for your flock? By flying? You can't fly *and* win the Challenge."

"What's the matter?" Kyp called back, climbing higher still. "Have you forgotten how to use your wings?"

"I'll catch you," Kuper grunted. "I'll catch you, and then I'll settle you, like I settled Kalum."

Abruptly, Kyp dropped and struck Kuper at the base of his spine. "*This* is for Kalum, who never treated you any way but well!" he said as he knocked Kuper sideways. "And *this* is for the Kinaar who you betrayed!" he said, striking with a forewing. "And *this*," he said, catching Kuper across the forehead with his beak, opening a cut over his right eye, "is for Kym."

Kuper lashed back with a talon. Kyp pivoted on the outstretched leg and came around behind him.

The tug sent Kuper tumbling, and Kyp landed on his back again. Two more quick strikes.

Kuper curled a forewing over against Kyp and leaned on him. Suddenly Kyp was supporting both his own weight as well as Kuper's. Then Kuper caught Kyp by the leg, gave a sudden jerk of his powerful neck muscles and flipped Kyp end over end. Kyp threw his wings out to regain balance, and Kuper came at him. For a moment, the two closed, and in the flurry, feathers drifted down to those of us watching below, their bodies so entangled that they almost appeared one thing.

From where we perched, watching anxiously, it seemed certain that the fight must go as everyone had feared — the smaller Crow tiring under the weight and press of the larger. Kuper thrust his talons at Kyp, but at that moment Kyp slipped to the left — a quick peck — and then he had tucked his wings close to his body and was dropping away. This sudden flight confused Kuper. He remembered all too well Kyp's escape back in the spring, but also he knew that Kyp was no coward. He couldn't believe he would flee in front of all the others. Besides, where could he possibly go, with Kuper's flock gathered in trees throughout the valley? Kuper flew after him.

A high, shrill screech suddenly ruptured the river basin. At the far end of the valley, drawing closer with each moment, was a long series of human boxes, hurtling forward. Kyp flew directly at it. Kuper attempted to cut him off, but Kyp was simply the better and faster flyer.

Kyp pulled up alongside the boxes. The noise, near as they were, became deafening. The heat generated by the boxes scorched their shoulders and wingtips. The smell and the smoke clawed at their throats. Kuper began to creep closer. Their feathers stirred under the hot breath from the roaring human boxes.

Kuper had maneuvered in behind Kyp, only two Crow lengths from him, and was considering how to continue the fight, close as they were to the boxes' crushing force. Then all at once, Kyp lifted one wing, rolled, dropped and was sucked underneath, directly into the heart and heat, noise and soot and darkness, where the madly spinning legs churned round and round.

Kuper grabbed air, curled over top and sought Kyp on the other side. But there was no sign of him.

The entire Collection rose into the air with a tremendous cry, crisscrossing above the pathway, searching for Kyp above and behind the human boxes. Some followed the human device closely, some trailed behind along the human trackway, scouring the tall grasses and low bushes that sprouted beside them. Those who followed stayed near until the boxes rushed, howling, headlong into the long black tunnel.

Though they searched the valley's entire length for a ruined body, a crushed carcass or a severed wing, and though they searched the riverbank and the trees — though no one believed he could possibly have made his way there — no sign or trace of Kyp was found. It was as if he had simply vanished.

Chapter 27

The sound of tumbling water filled the gorge. We had found our way to the tiny high-sided ravine Kyp had suggested to Erkala. The cliffs soared to a narrow slot above us, so we were nearly invisible to anyone flying overhead, and our speech was masked by the brook's clamor in this confined space. We all perched upon rocks and within bushes, sprayed by the cascading stream's foam, and waited.

When Kyp finally slid over the lip of the cliffs, a shout went up from the entire band. He fell more than landed on a perch among the rocks, then sat quietly a moment before asking, "Are we all here?"

I nodded. "You were right. The moment the Challenge began, the others entirely forgot about us. We were able to slip away without anyone noticing — but can I just say *I* had the most difficult time tearing myself from that competition." And though I knew what a serious situation we all found ourselves in, I couldn't help but laugh. "Ah, *that*," I told him, as he began methodically rearranging his feathers, "*that* was some beautiful planning. *That* was thinking like a Crow. Leaving them hanging, searching for you on the ground and through the tall grasses as you were whistled away clinging to the bottom of that noisy, smoky human box."

For only the second time I had seen, Erkala laughed out loud. "That big one — now *he* will be upset for a good many days."

"Oh yes," I said, still chuckling. "And wasn't that some clever flying? Kyp, *what* have I told you? Your hummingbird for color. Your hawk for speed. And for elegance of flight, and style and grace — the Crow. *That* will be a story I can repeat when my chicks' chicks have chicks. Isn't that so, everyone?" The rest of the band cheered their approval.

Kyp cocked his head and peered at me. "*If* you have chicks," he replied before becoming more serious. "But Kuper chided me, saying I was no Chooser. And he was right. I'm not your Chooser. I wasn't Chosen. I've never finished training. I left the only Clan that might have wanted me to Choose, and where has all my good advice led you, but to this hidden cliffside roost fit for a flock of swallows."

"Maybe," I agreed, "if you forget that your advice saved our lives. A long time ago I told you that inviting others to join you and me would only cause us trouble. And I was right! It seems that there hasn't been anything but trouble. But it looks to me like we're stuck with one another. And *you*, my friend — you are the closest thing we have to a Chooser."

"So," Kaf asked, direct as always, "now what?"

"If you would continue to listen to me," Kyp said and sighed, "I would advise that we leave."

Kyf looked up from nibbling on a mushroom she'd discovered. "When?"

Kyp settled his feathers and lifted his head. "Right away."

"And go where?" Kyrt asked. "You're right. We have to leave. That Collector one will be angry, and he won't wait to look for us. He'll be sending out scouts. He already knows a little about the direction we're heading."

"The best thing we can do then," Kyp said, "is to take a different direction."

"What do you mean?" Kaf asked.

"We'll fly east first. Then south."

"East?" Kyf objected. "That would take us over open water. And in bad weather."

"That's right," Kyp allowed. "They'll look along the coast, but they won't think to travel out on the water. I would put as much distance between Kuper and the rest of that bunch as we can. And I wouldn't wait for daylight."

"You mean leave tonight?"

"I mean now."

Everyone considered their tired wings, empty stomachs and the snow that slithered over the ravine's edge. Then Erkala skipped to a perch on the edge of a branch. "Good," she said and turned to the others. "Shouldn't we go?"

The band responded with a flurry of wings. Moments later, we had set out over the ocean.

Cousins, you know me well enough to know that I am no coward, but there are things I wouldn't willingly enter once, let alone twice. Before I revisit this wing of the journey, I must drink and rest my voice. If you've cached food, eat it, and we'll meet back shortly.

Part Three

chapter 28

Close in, and settle where you can.

For many of you — most of you — a good part of this story is unknown. If the account is too painful to take in a single hearing, forgive me for not having shared something of it with you earlier. I'm only now able to return to it. I have had to remind myself of the hard lesson learned by Great Crow in his journey to find Sun Eagle — sometimes we must travel through darkness to arrive at light.

In any case, draw close.

We set out across the ocean. Light snow continued to fall. This, we knew, would be helpful to us. Any tracks or signs left at our perch in the ravine would soon be covered.

Kyp chose to fly low, just above the surf's spray. We lost something in terms of visibility — the higher you fly, the farther you are able to see. But, of course, the higher you fly, the more likely you are to be seen. Flying low as we were, the Collection would have difficulty spotting us. There was also this — if you have to fly any distance, and need to ration your energy, there is strength and ease in flying close to the water. Watch your pelicans and the other large sea birds — when they travel, they fly so close it seems they are almost touching the surface. For some reason the Maker supports you most when you move closest to her.

We flew at a steady speed, straight east. The sky cleared briefly just before moonrise, and it was by that light that we altered our course and turned south and west. Then cloud cover rolled back in. The snow began falling again around the middle of the dark six. Soon it was snowing heavily.

It's possible to navigate by moonlight, starlight or the lights that humans generate, but we'd lost moonlight and starlight when cloud cover returned, and the humans' lights along the shore winked out as the storm strengthened. Now we found ourselves in the uncomfortable and dangerous position of having to fly through total darkness.

Even so, it's possible to maintain direction if you keep your wits. The prevailing wind tells you something. The sound of the surf as it strikes landfall tells you something. Erkala knew as much as anyone about flying over open water, so she positioned herself next to Kyp, and they conferred as we flew.

It was a long flight, and a hard flight, through most of the night, and under the worst possible conditions. We were already dead tired from our escape. The darkness closed in tight, and it became difficult to hold on to any sense of direction, even up or down. The surf surged high and caught the tips of our wings. The snow hissed down, small, icy and pebble hard.

Then, all at once, out of the darkness and snow, in the middle of open water, a dim, cold light emerged, blue and pale at first, then gradually growing brighter. As if climbing out of the water, an immense human figure rose, brandishing fire in its paw. As we drew closer, it became clear that it stood astride a small island.

Then the sheets of snow parted and there, just beyond the monstrous human figure, glittered a vast, sweeping stretch of coastline pieced together entirely of specks of light. One soaring human roost after another, stacked upon one another, piled next to one another — more than one could possibly count.

Our flight slowed as we took in the sheer scale of that human colony. I flew up alongside Kyp.

"Which way?" I shouted over the surf.

"We need shelter in this weather," he shouted back. "We can't perch between the rocks by the shore. We'll search for a roost." He nodded at the lights. "In there. There must be trees somewhere."

In no time, it seemed, we were in among the humans.

Imagine, all the humans you have ever seen. Now triple that, and triple it again, and crush them into one towering stony roost. Then line up thousands of these roosts. Thousands of roosts. Millions of humans. Humans oozing from roosts. Humans thronging between the stone canyons. Humans and human things for as far as the spirit can imagine.

The glare was dizzying, confusing and frightening. Each light seemed to beckon us to escape from the darkness, but each led to a new danger — a stone treetop, invisible stone barriers or rushing human boxes. Kyp's voice rose above the din of the wind and the humans — the flock had to stay together and avoid staring at the lights. I knew from my experience among humans that the lights were dangerous. It was easy to become bewildered and dash up against the glittering surfaces.

But how to avoid looking at the lights? They were everywhere. Draped from the ends of sticks. Strung like berries on vines through the middle of the canyons. Projecting from the top of human roosts. Glaring out through the glossy, invisible stones.

We steered a course through the middle of the canyons, and Kyp's chant became ours: "Stay in the middle, stay in the middle." Avoid the lines and snares erected everywhere. Eventually the throbbing lights caused a sickness of the spirit and a fever of the brain. Shortly after we entered the human's colony, tired beyond caring, dazed and bemused by the lights, Kych and Kynwyt turned directly into and were broken against a human roost.

Sometimes the Truth is too big or too terrible to describe. This portion of the journey was like that. Tired beyond tired, we flew past what became an infinity of identical towering human roosts. Rock seemed to cover everything. Humans swarmed from their roosts like ants swarming from anthills. Deep in the heart of the human colony, the lights seemed alive. They moved and shifted, climbed the cliffs, crawled up along the sides. Images of humans appeared to stride across their stoneworks from one roost to another, monstrously large, hideously bright, bigger than the biggest creature ever seen. Huge human faces — some as high as mountains — their mouths gaping, with immense, gleaming teeth. All lit by some inner fire. And everywhere, everywhere, everywhere beneath us — *real* humans teemed, shouted, scrambled across the surface, called to one another. Path upon path upon path was choked by humans and their rushing, roaring, smoke-spewing human boxes.

Kyp guided us through the valleys, avoided watching the lights, maintained a steady head, cajoled us to continue when we felt we couldn't. He coaxed us to fly higher, just above the tops of the roosts, where the lights had less influence, where we felt less confused and disoriented. But there — high up, half in darkness, half in light, blown by the storm, frozen by the snow — we reached the end of our reserves.

Had we flown even a short while longer, who knows how things might have ended? But, miraculously, in the middle of all that human horror and human noise and crush and chaos — trees! Maker, what a sight. Not just one or two, the way humans normally arrange things, but thousands, and great thriving elders among them. Craggy oaks and soaring elms, beeches and birches and willows. Old trees, gnarled trees, raising up their branches in welcome. Kyp promptly gave the call, and we descended.

The snow still fell. It swirled and swept past and through those woods. The branches shivered and the trees swayed. The night sky pressed close, heavy, gray clouds hanging down. But after the confusion of the false canyons and blinding lights, the branches beneath our talons felt real and comforting and reassuringly solid.

I tucked my head under a wing, as much to shelter myself from the relentless sounds of the humans as for warmth, closed my eyes and fell fast asleep.

chapter 29

The sun rose.

I woke, felt light warming my neck and heard a stirring within the roost. I opened my eyes and saw Kyp squinting up at the sun's on-again, off-again attempt to pierce the clouds. Small feather-light pellets of snow still skittered through the branches.

I stretched my wings. "Are any of the others awake yet?"

"None," he said, stamping his talons. "They're all still exhausted from last night's flight."

I scanned the stand of trees. As light filtered through branches, the glade gradually warmed. It was an even bigger forest than I had understood in the night. In addition to all the large oaks, elm and maples, there were a surprising number of needle bearers — spruce, pine and fir. A delicate stream twisted and trickled past boulders and between small rises, and a little ways down, a tiny pond wedged itself neatly into the lowest end of the valley.

The snow that had fallen the previous night glistened and glittered, caught by the light. A breeze stirred the trees, and nearly invisible clouds of the lightest, driest snow and ice crystals wafted shimmering through the air.

I looked at the branches spreading about us. "This is a good tree. It has long roots and a strong spine. In another time and place I might have been happy to select this as a Gathering Tree."

Kyp nodded. "This was all good land once. You can still see the bones and claws of it here and there, but humans have dug it over, thrown it up and created as barren a desert as you'll ever find. This is the only island of real life in it."

"Plenty of good eating, though," I pointed out. "Humans can be counted on to leave gifts for the quick."

He grunted his agreement. Farther over on the ground, two humans ambled across a snow-covered field, and a scattering of pigeons pecked at the remains of human leftovers, their rhythmic cooing seeming suddenly loud.

"Plenty of pigeons," I observed.

"Pigeons, pah." Kyp clacked his beak in disgust. "What a wreck humans have made of them. First Time Pigeons may not have been the smartest birds in creation, but now they're barely even birds. Look at them! Pecking and bobbing and nodding between the legs of the human."

Kyp stared a long time at the pigeons, listening to their soft, relentless thrumming. "That's what we could become if we stayed among humans, stealing from them as Kuper wants. Eventually. Just another kind of pigeon, pecking in and out of the human's paws. We have to escape that."

He stretched his wings. "It's a shame," he concluded, "but there you have it. This was once something wonderful — but humans have changed it into a place fit only for pigeons."

"And rats," a voice added. We turned and realized that Erkala had awakened. "I saw several scamper between the rocks along the edge of the lake."

"*And* rats," Kyp agreed sourly.

We perched, lost in our own private thoughts, dusted by snow. When we returned from our thoughts, the human colony remained, a jagged, ominous-seeming, stone-gray landscape.

"I had no idea, before I came here," Kyp said, to no one in particular. "No idea of the size." Then he turned to us. "Now," he said, shaking his head, the enormity of it all striking him. "Where are we to look?"

Chapter 30

It was a good question. Where to begin? And how to proceed once we'd started?

The flock provided a partial answer. Shortly after Kyrt awoke, he approached Kyp. "You brought us safe through the humans, away from the Collection and across the water. Now we can do our part. Divided up," he said, gesturing to his band, "we can cover territory quickly. Just tell us what you want us to look for."

Kyf had been itching to organize the yearlings from the time she'd first laid eyes on them. Now she seized the opportunity. By the day's end, she'd put a system into place and the teams had set out.

The winter passed according to the rigid schedule

of Kyf's invention: Each day as the sun rose, the flock would leave the roost, fly out in pairs to find forage and then look for Kym. We approached the sprawling human rookery canyon by canyon, south to north. Hunting at ground level first, we proceeded up, keeping our eyes open as we rose. Where we encountered jays or ravens, we questioned them. Had they seen anything of a captive Crow, we asked. A Crow who could speak with humans? Before nightfall we would return to the roost, report to Kyf and share information and scavenge if we had it.

If Kyp, Kyf, Kaf, Kwaku, Erkala or I weren't too tired, we took turns teaching the yearlings the things Crows learn when they fly with Family: where to find food, which trees make the best roost, where to place scouts, how to build a nest.

We slowly learned what it meant to share territory with the humans on this scale. There were hazards specific to this place: cats, a certain level of constant, irritating noise. Scrupulous attention had to be paid to scavenge. Three of the yearlings — Kwykat, Kwytynat and Kynakut — succumbed to poison.

By mid-winter we had begun to act a little like a genuine flock — but we still hadn't come across the slightest sign of Kym. As winter deepened, storms swept in. Each day, there was some new route to explore. Each day we arrived back at the roost with the same answer: No sign.

After one particularly cold and blustery session of searching, Kyp returned to the tree late. Most of the flock had already retired.

He listened to the throb that we had become accustomed to — the roar of the humans' boxes, the hum of their conversation. Erkala perched beside him. "Good eating," she said.

"The wind under your wings," he replied absently. They studied the winking lights and the slow, restless movements of humans.

"It's late," Erkala observed.

He nodded. "And the Maker only knows what we're doing here." He stamped his talons to warm them, then abruptly kicked a piece of ice to the ground below. Instantly he regretted his outburst and glanced up and around at the sleeping figures perched in branches throughout the tree. "All these poor Crows," he said at last. "What have I put them through?"

"You put us through nothing," Erkala corrected him. "You guided us out of a number of hard situations and found a place for us here."

"Yes," he agreed. "I've brought you here. And what credit does that do me?"

Erkala cocked her head and studied Kyp a moment. "Others would have given up, that's true," she allowed, "but Katakata says many times we should dream true, and of all the Crows I see, you alone have never wavered in your dream. Look at those who follow you now. Not one related to you. Not one follows you for any reason but the quality of your dreams." Her gaze lingered on the tree's upper reaches a moment, then she said in a lower voice, "No one knows their Life Test. That cannot be revealed until the Maker is ready. Everything in life is preparation for that event. But there are many of the … in my old tongue we call it 'Taku.' It means 'when the owl turns away.'"

"I'm not sure I understand. I don't think we have a word for that."

"Maybe not," Erkala allowed after considering it a moment. "It means any time you make a decision, or do something that may end up getting you eaten … and it doesn't. They are tests to prepare us for when the Maker calls us." She looked at Kyp. "This journey of yours was Taku. Believe it. And you passed."

Chapter 31

How many needles project from the branches and twigs in a pine forest? How many pebbles lie scattered in the rocky drifts and slides of a mountain slope? Study snow as it swirls through a blizzard and see if you can count the flakes. Though the band left the roost each day with a ready will, it seemed at times that we had not even begun to touch the number of human nests in this colony.

It was shortly after the time when days begin to grow longer that Kyp returned from searching and tiredly set down on a perch. Kyf had become accustomed to greeting teams as they settled onto the branches, to learn what had been discovered and to pass it along as quickly as possible.

She dropped beside Kyp.

"Anything?" she asked.

Kyp shook his head.

"Are you hungry?"

"A little," Kyp replied half-heartedly.

"Then come eat," she called and flew past him.

Wearily he spread his wings and leaped from the branch. "How far?" he called after her.

"A short flight," she shouted back, turning east in the direction of the coast.

After flying for what seemed a considerable time, Kyp drew up alongside Kyf. "It's late," he objected. "I'll find scavenge nearer the roost."

She shook her head. "Only a little farther."

They arrived at the coast, and there, perched on an upright log projecting from the water, was one of the yearlings, Kwykwyatyn.

"Good eating," he greeted them.

"Show him," Kyf commanded.

"Show me what?" Kyp asked.

"There," he said, gesturing with an upraised talon straight ahead.

"What kind of scavenge can I find here?" Kyp was asking — and then stopped.

A human roost of medium size overlooked the water. Like most of the roosts in this territory, it had several layers — eight to this one. On the fourth layer, a number of holes were lit from within, all covered and obstructed by the human's invisible stone. Through the invisible stone it was possible to see three regularly shaped flat rocks, and on each one sat a kind of weave, and in each one perched a solitary, confined Crow.

Chapter 32

Kyp flew to the edge of the human roost, perched on a rocky ledge outside the fourth layer opening and looked inside. He tapped at the invisible barrier. Close as he was now, he could see that the roost was crowded with Crows, all separated from one another. The Crows, disturbed by the knocking, stirred on their perches and turned their heads.

One of them stared directly at him and stood. "Kyp?"

"Kym? Is it you?"

They stood, frozen, for a long, long time. Kyp took a single step forward and pressed his beak to the clear stone.

"How," Kym asked, "did you find me?"

"I don't know. I've had help, but even now it doesn't seem possible. The Maker must have directed me." He made a move then that he was to repeat several times during their conversation. Forgetting the barrier, he attempted to move closer, bumped into it and then stepped back. "How are you?" he asked.

"I'm good," she answered. "They feed me — all of us — regularly."

The other Crows in the room had turned to look and listen. A ripple of conversation ran through them.

"Who is that one?" someone called from farther back.

"What is he saying?" called another.

"He's from my Flock," Kym replied, then raised her voice to be heard over the clamor. "Now hush and let me talk."

Kyp craned his neck to peer as far as he might into the roost. "What is this place?" he asked. "Why have they brought you here?"

"I don't know. But they have more than fifty Crows in here, and a talonful of jays, magpies and ravens."

Kyp pressed flat against the stone and tried to peer as closely into the roost as he could with his right eye. From where he was, he could count fifty-seven birds. Each bird was held within a thing woven together like a magpie's nest, but a magpie's nest has a way in and out, and this seemed to be all weave and no entrance.

Kyp cocked his head. "What exactly is that thing you're perched in?"

"It's what they keep us in," Kym said and made a strange sound at the back of her throat. "That's what they call it, I think."

"Well, I'm less interested in what they call it than how they get you out. How did they put you in it? I don't see a hole. Did they build it around you?"

"No. They do something. With their paws — here." She gestured with her beak at a spot in the construction. "They tug on something, and an opening appears."

Kyp turned his head to observe it with his left eye. "You mean, magically?"

"No, it's like the flap on a spider's hole. It's attached and falls into place. Somehow it's hooked over something, and then it slides up."

Kyp crouched to get a better look. "They just … pull … on something?"

"That's it."

"Show me where again."

Kym leaned forward and pushed at the weave with a talon. "It's this part. You see how the strand here is slightly thicker?"

"Yes."

"That's what slides up."

"Do they ever take you out?"

"Sometimes," Kym allowed. "To stick things into us."

Kyp tried to keep his shock from showing. "To *stick* things into you?" he repeated. "What sorts of things?"

"Sharp things. Like thorns. One human holds you," she answered matter-of-factly, "the other one pokes it in."

Kyp stared at her and tried to collect his thoughts. "Why?" he asked finally.

"For blood."

"How's that?" Kyp asked, so startled by the answer he was unable to disguise his surprise.

"They take blood from us," Kym answered and sighed tiredly. "It's not as bad as it sounds. It doesn't last long. Once they've taken it, they leave us alone. Other than that, they never let us out."

Kyp struggled to keep his growing agitation in check. He stepped stiffly to the edge of the perch, then returned to the invisible stone and pressed his head as close as he could.

"I'm going to leave for a little while," he said at last. "I have to talk with some others. But listen to me, I'm coming back and we're going to get you out of there."

She stared through the strands of her weave. "How?"

"I don't know. But we'll find a way." He scanned the roost again. "Where are they? I don't see any humans."

"They aren't here all the time. They leave each day prior to the dark six. Seem to come for five days, then stay away for two. That's not always the way, but pretty much."

Kyp tapped at the invisible stone. "These ... barriers. I've seen humans meddle with them. Do they ever open these?"

"No. In all the time I've been here, I've never seen them opened. I don't think they can be."

"What about talking to the humans, Kym? You know their language. Can't you say something to them?"

Suddenly she looked very tired and shook her head, "Oh, Kyp. It's so much harder than I thought. There are so many words I can't understand. I'm only starting to see how much I don't know. There's something they do with their faces. It's a bit like the way we can call to our folk with our bodies. We can deliver the Call to Roost without words. Humans do something like that all the time with their faces. But I don't know how. I don't know if we will ever really talk with them. And I don't know what to do." She rested her forehead against the weave a moment. "I've spent my time in here thinking, thinking. Thinking about how to help these Crows. Thinking about how to escape. But I can't ... I can't figure how to get out of here. I've begun to believe that I never will."

Kyp tapped sharply at the barrier and Kym raised her head. "Listen to me," he said. "I haven't flown all this way to ..." Words escaped him. He stopped, then started again quietly. "When we fly from here, Kym, that weave you're in won't matter. These invisible stones won't matter. You'll be with us. We'll find a way to get you out. We will."

chapter 33

The next morning, early, just before sunrise, Kyp fetched me from forage. He led me to the newly discovered human roost, showed me where the Crows were confined and pointed Kym out to me. I congratulated him, but he waved it away and directed my attention to the weaves that held the Crows.

"Those things," I asked, "what are they?"

"It's like the magpie who got away told you. They're woven something like a swallow's nest — see, look, it opens there." A human moved close to one of the weaves, and after grasping it in some way, it stuck its paw in.

I craned my head to see what it was doing, but

my view was blocked by its enormous back. All at once, it was holding a jay in its paw.

"How did it do that?" I asked.

"There's an opening that's covered. That human must have twisted something, one of those branches, and made them come apart." Kyp turned his head to me. "I have a favor to ask of you. I need you to spend some time watching them."

The human had done something to the jay and now placed it back within the weave. "And then?" I asked.

"Find out how they make the weaves open."

"I see," I answered, although I wasn't sure how I could discover its magic from this distance.

"And then —" he continued.

"And *then*? There's more?"

"I want you to find out how *we* can do that. When I go in there, I'll have to know what the trick is, or else … it'll all have been useless." His eyes roved across the weaves and the Crows perched within them, then he fixed his gaze on me. "Kata, you more than anyone else I know understand how to get in and out of things. I need you to do this."

Suddenly the human turned. It opened its fleshy mouth and released a low warbling grunt. Within moments, another human had lumbered into the roost. Both stared sullenly at us, pointed and cautiously approached.

Kyp and I leaped into the air. As we made our way back to the tree, Kyp turned to me. "Watch them, Kata, and talk to Kym — she's been watching them. Find a way to open those things. You're the thief — do what comes naturally to you."

Chapter 34

How does the saying go? "You have to fly with your eyes open if you want to find your roost." Now I flew with my eyes open.

When I grew tired of watching and waiting for a human to come and take a Crow out, I flew through the endless stone canyons, gazed down on humans and studied how they lived. Looking at them, really *looking* at them, I *saw* humans as if I was seeing them for the first time.

I saw how they lived and began to understand the meaning of the distinct roosts that they kept. I saw how humans separated everything out. How they maintained some spaces for eating, some spaces for sleeping, some spaces for cleaning themselves and some for activities that I'm still not able to describe or comprehend. I saw the relationship they had with their usual slaves — your dogs and cats — but I learned just how many other animals were confined within that teeming human colony. Parrots and parakeets, finches and canaries, fishes and ferrets and spiders and lizards, mice and even snakes. It occurred to me that there was nothing that existed, nothing moving and breathing and living, that humans didn't need to capture and confine.

And I discovered something else. Something that surprised me. Along with all the separate spaces that humans created, there appeared to be parts of the human colony set aside for nothing but the confinement and display of animals — most of them behind weaves like the one Kym found herself in. All of the Maker's animals captured and confined, crammed into tiny roosts, waiting for something to pry open their weaves.

Mostly when I peered in, I was quiet and well hidden, and the animals didn't see me. I tried, as I watched, to find out how the confinement worked and how one could spring the trap that had snared them. But on the few occasions that the animals caught sight of me, I could see them stare back, at *me* — on the other side of the invisible barrier, on the other side of the weave — free. Then a hopeless, hungry, heartsick expression would appear behind their eyes, an expression so powerful, so filled with longing and regret and loss, that I would have to turn and leave.

chapter 35

Kym opened her eyes. "Who are you?" she asked as she slowly wakened. An unusual-looking Crow peered through the invisible stone.

The visitor moved closer. "Erkala," she replied. "I've come to see how many there are in here."

"Kyp knows that already," Kym mumbled sleepily as she stretched and rose to her talons. "Fifty-seven."

"I wanted to check for myself," Erkala replied, craned her head and squinted beyond Kym. "Is this the only roost? There aren't Crows down the side passages?"

"I don't think so. I've never seen any others. We've never heard anyone else."

Erkala continued looking. "Kyp said there were birds of other kinds here."

"That's right. Magpies, jays and ravens."

"How are they all?"

Kym scanned the confines. "Some better than others. We talk. Try to keep our spirits up. Behave as much like a flock as we can. Some grow silent or give up hope. One of the ravens — each day he refused food and plucked out feathers. He died ten days ago."

"Do humans have much to do with you?"

"Not much. They come. Look at us. Change the water."

"And take blood from you?"

"Kyp told you that?" Kym asked. Erkala nodded. "I know it sounds bad, but it's not that painful. They stick these things, like the nose of a mosquito, only longer and bigger, into your body, through the skin. It hurts only for a moment. They pull something, like a tail, at its end. And the blood is sucked in."

Erkala stilled a shudder. "Why?"

Kym shook her head. "I don't know. It sounds horrible. I've thought about it a lot, but I don't know what the answer is. Every one of us in here has had the Plague and survived. It's the only thing we have in common. I can't help but think it has to have something to do with that. Who knows? Maybe they drink it to keep the Plague from their own nests."

Erkala stared. "You're very brave."

"Am I?" Kym turned and faced Erkala directly. "I feel the opposite of brave. I feel like I am living a dream — but not one of our dreams, not even one of the Maker's dreams, but a strange human dream. Somewhere, someplace, a human has dreamed all of this. These other birds, these roosts, these walls, these weaves."

The intensity of Kym's gaze was so strong, Erkala was compelled to look away. "I have had that kind of feeling, too," Erkala replied at last. "And I don't believe in false hope. The Maker tests us, and sometimes the tests are more than we are capable of. But the Maker is also mysterious. If she wants something to change, it can happen in an instant and it won't matter what is in the way."

"Do you believe that?" Kym asked.

"I *know* that," Erkala answered. Though there seemed little else to say, she hesitated, as if there was still something that needed attending to.

"What?" Kym asked.

"I have," Erkala said, pressing closer to the invisible barrier, "one other question."

"Yes?"

"These Crows that are here, with you," Erkala began. "I understand they have been collected from many places. Some from very far."

"That's true." Kym nodded. "Some of their

languages are so different I have trouble understanding them."

"Are there," Erkala asked, her voice dropping so low Kym had to lean in to hear, "any that *look* different?"

"Different?"

Erkala raised her head. "That look like me?"

Kym studied Erkala closely through the invisible barrier, then slowly shook her head. "No," she said, "I'm sorry. None."

"Don't be sorry. It doesn't matter. I was just curious. I'll tell Kyp what I found out, and —"

"Has anyone," Kym interrupted before Erkala could turn away, "found a way in or out of this roost?"

"Not yet. But if anyone can, it would be Kyp."

chapter 36

Everyone's duties changed as we focused on finding a way into the fourth layer of this human roost. Kyf threw herself into reorganizing the flock. She had discovered that the yearlings worked best if the tasks were designed as games, and now she set them to work at a different kind of hide-and-seek. Each day we flew around the human structure. We probed the surface of the roost, explored the upper reaches, where narrow stone tunnels stuck up, examined the entrances at ground level, where the humans streamed in and out. We studied how long the entrances were left open, how they were shut and which human shut them. We considered tiny cracks and pulled at any piece of the roost that seemed loose or crumbling. We did all that … and found nothing.

The next morning we woke up, fed and did the same thing.

One day, late in the mid-sixth, we rested on a tiny, resilient beech that grew near the squat, brooding human roost. Kyf had returned with a flattened, squishy human scavenge that was sprinkled with thin strips of meat, and she shared it with us. We tore at it, while the wind gusted, thrusting a rattling mixture of discarded human things, dust and gritty snow along. Each of us fluffed our feathers to keep the warm air close to our skin. The cooing and thrumming of pigeons that we'd grown so accustomed to wafted up to our perch.

Abruptly, Kyp dropped his scavenge, leaped to the ground and brusquely scattered the pigeons, who quickly fled, sounding more offended than frightened.

"What was that all about?" I asked when Kyp returned.

"I don't like having them around," he objected sourly. "I can't stand looking at them."

Kaf, Kwaku and Erkala exchanged glances.

"It's not the pigeons," Kyp said after a few moments. "It's just … It's so …" He nodded over at the human roost. "There it is. Right there. We travel to this spot each day and do exactly the same thing —

fly around it, search for openings. But there *are* none. There are no openings but the ones the humans use. There are no holes, no gaps, no breaks. It's no wonder everyone is getting restless — I'm restless and *I'm* the one who brought us here! I'm so frustrated I could chew stone and spit pebbles!"

Kyp raised his head and looked up at the fourth layer opening. "It's almost a moon since we found Kym. Almost a moon — it will be spring soon — and I'm no closer to getting her out now than I was when we arrived. I can't leave, but I can't expect everyone to stay with me indefinitely."

"No one is keeping us here," Erkala said quietly. "We're here, all of us, because we want to be."

"And I appreciate that." Kyp drew a long, deep breath. Then he turned to me. "Kata, are you any closer to discovering how to open the weave?"

Caught with my beak full, I quickly swallowed before speaking. "Kym and I are fairly certain we understand how it's done. The humans pull something, and that allows them to slide a section away. How *we* can do that ..." I didn't know what to say. "We're working on it," I concluded.

Kyp next turned to Kyf. "Has anyone come up with a way to get into the roost? Anyone seen anything and told you?"

"No," Kyf answered matter-of-factly. "Nothing."

Kyp flapped his wings in frustration. "How? *How*

can we get in? There has to be a way. First we have to find some way into the roost. *Then* we have to find our way to the roost's fourth layer, where the Crows are kept. *Then* we have to find a way to get Kym out of the weave and out of the roost. The easiest way in would be to shatter the invisible stone — but it's too hard. We've seen that. Crows hurt themselves on it all the time. We can't peck through. There are no holes to *crawl* through. Maker in the Roost," he finished wearily, "why bring us all this distance if there's no way of getting in?"

"You're not thinking like a Crow," Kwaku said calmly. "Breaking through. Pecking through. Maybe a woodpecker would do that. That's not what the Maker would expect us to do. You will have to *think* your way in — the moment you start thinking like a *Crow*, the way will become as plain as bark on a branch."

"Yes. Well." Kyp composed himself. "I'd be happy if *you'd* start thinking like a Crow for me. It would seem that my head's too small."

Suddenly Erkala interrupted. "Maybe it's not a matter of thinking like a Crow at all. *They* have a way in."

"Who?" Kyp asked, looking about.

"*Them*," she said, nodding at the waterfront. "The rats. Look! They enter there, in their tunnels by the shore. Sometimes they come out in the gravel on the other side of the roost. They must travel underneath."

"Maybe," Kyp allowed, "but how do we know they go into the roost?"

"I know rats." Erkala was as excited as I'd ever heard her. "If there is food above, and warmth, believe me, *they* have found a way. If they dig beneath the roost, they *must* climb up too."

"It's possible," Kaf cautiously agreed.

"Come," Erkala called, already flying to look.

We flew to the other side of the building farthest from the river, where a rock-strewn mound had been thrown up.

"Now watch," she said.

It wasn't long before the tan and gray fur of a pigeon-sized rat was seen scrambling through the gravel. The rat nosed about briefly, then disappeared.

"This way!" Erkala beckoned and — with the rest of us behind her — returned to the tree we'd been perched in. We stared at the small tunnel's mouth. Nothing.

Kaf cleared his throat. "Those tunnels could lead anywhere —"

Suddenly a ripple appeared in the water that trickled from the tunnel out onto the shore. The water scattered and broke, and the dark, moist tip of a rat's nose surfaced.

"That one! See? *That* is the same one we saw on the other side."

"You're sure?" Kyp asked, thinking, like myself, that they all looked pretty much alike.

"Certain! There is a scar on its right ear."

"Is it possible there are other rat holes at the base of the dwelling? Ones that go up?" Kyp asked.

Erkala was already away. "Let's look!" she called.

As they flew to explore the rat warren further, something else caught my eye. Something bright. For a moment it glinted as intensely as the sun, only coming from much, much lower.

A human walked on the ground about three trees from me. As it turned its head to look at something, I saw the glitter wink at me again. What was it? I followed the human, flying from tree to tree, watching.

Then an amazing thing happened. The human sat under a tree, reached up a paw and lifted the shiny thing up. It held the thing — no bigger than a butterfly's wing — beneath its nose, where it could look at it. Then it rubbed the side of its head, took the shiny thing and stuck it back, just beneath its right ear.

The Maker had led me to this spot and revealed this to me for a reason, I was certain. When the human stood and began walking again, I followed.

Chapter 37

It was late in the final sixth when I returned to the roost. Everyone had retired to a perch. Some were already sleeping. Kyp, Kwaku, Kyf and Kaf were talking near the trunk at the high end of an oak when I dropped onto the branch next to them. "This is how the weave will be opened," I announced and held up my prize.

"What are you talking about?" Kaf asked.

"What *is* that?" Kyf demanded, craning her head to look.

"I don't know what they call it," I said, placing it carefully on the branch. "It's a human's thing — they hang it from their ear. But — I was up at the human's roost watching them, just to make sure — if you hold it in your beak and stick the curvy end down into the human weave, so that it hooks around the twig holding things in place, and then pull it back up … I talked it over with Kym, and we agreed. *This* should do it. *This* should open the weave."

Kyp bent over the shiny thing to have a better look. "You really think so?"

I nodded. "Yes."

Kyp picked it up in his beak, then passed it down to his talons and shook it. "Can you teach me how it works?"

I leaned over and plucked it back. "Why?"

"So I can open the weave when I get in, of course."

"No, no," I said as I set the prize aside. "It's too … It's too complicated. I think this is probably something I will have to do myself. So I'll come with you."

Kyp shook his head. "No, no. This is for *me* to do." He stepped over, seized the shiny thing once again and placed it near his talons. "I can't ask anyone else to do that."

I snatched it back and sat on it. "But you don't *have* to ask, and I think this is something you will need my help with. I'm not going to have this thing misused and wasted just because you don't know how to make it work."

"I think you're making a fuss over nothing," Kyp retorted, his feathers flaring briefly, "but we don't have to decide right away. We still haven't figured how to get into the roost."

"Well. That's not entirely true," Erkala disagreed softly as she dropped to the branch.

Kyp turned to her. "You've worked it out?"

"I've just returned from the waterfront. The rats definitely have a tunnel that leads up and into the roost."

"And you think they'll allow me to use their tunnels?"

"You? No." Erkala snorted derisively and shook her head. "Me? I think so, yes. And they might allow me to invite a few others."

Kyp turned his head back and forth between us. "I can't do it. I can't ask you to come."

"You guided us out of the trap and past the humans," she said. "I'm not concerned about climbing into this roost with you."

"If it's a question of who's going and who's not," Kwaku said slowly, "I think I'd better come, too."

"Why?" Kyp asked.

"I don't know, exactly," Kwaku replied, pressing a wayward feather into place, "but I dreamed of the four of us working our way through that human roost. In my dream, somehow, it was important for me to be with you. I don't really care for tunnels or rats, or human roosts for that matter, but it would seem to be a poor time for me to start ignoring my dreams."

Kyp peered at Kwaku. "Have you asked your brother and sister about this?"

"They already know I'm going," he said as he watched his feather spring back up. "I told them a day ago."

"I see," Kyp said and then sat silently.

"Well," he began again after a moment, "I always thought I would go in alone. It still feels like it's too much for me to ask. But for some reason, it appears we're meant to do this together. If Kwaku saw it, then ..." He shook his head. "I don't understand it, really. But I can't say that I'll be sad to have your company."

Kyf leaned up against Kwaku and laid her head on his shoulder. We remained silent for a long time. Then I recalled something. "Kwaku, back in the valley before the Collector and his flock arrived, you were telling a story."

He looked surprised that I remembered it. "Yes?"

"It's not a story I had heard before. How does it end?"

"It's late," he objected, "and I'm not sure I remember where I was in the telling."

"The Maker," Erkala recalled as she settled into a comfortable spot on the branch, "the Maker had just returned."

Kwaku looked at her. "Right. There's not much more to the end." Seeing that we all were waiting to hear it, he began. "The Maker looked about at the world. Bushes all gone. Trees all gone. All under water. Even the mountains covered. Finally, the rain stopped. The Maker examined the water closely. There was the human, tying reeds and making them float. There was Otter swimming, pulling up kelp. And Great Crow, he was there, too. Hopping from one piece of driftwood to another and stealing from everyone.

"The Maker looked about and realized then — after all that rain and all that trouble — that the creatures hadn't disappeared. There were just fewer of them. She shook her head at their stubbornness and their willfulness and their tremendous strength, and she laughed out loud and said, 'Better let them be.'

"And she spoke in a louder voice, said 'Let it get dry,' and all that water started to go away. The mountaintops began peeking out, and she summoned every surviving creature to the summit of one of those dry mountains, gathered them about her and told them, 'There's only one beginning. We don't get a chance to begin again in this world, so everyone's going to have to work harder to make things right.'

"And she flew away — the last time she would appear to all the creatures on Earth — calling back over her shoulder, 'The world won't get better on its own, so you'd best get busy.'"

When Kwaku was finished the story, he, Kyp and Kyf flew away to meet with Kyrt and Kaf to discuss how to organize the band. I was left alone with Erkala. The human roost rose up in my thoughts again, squat, dark and threatening. I hadn't liked it when I first saw it. I liked it even less knowing I would be going in.

Erkala perched calmly on the branch next to me, preening.

"So?" I asked. "This is the way we are going in? Underground? It's forbidden, of course."

"And yet, Great Crow entered Badger's den when it became necessary," Erkala replied. She looked at me in that way she has, as though she was looking straight into me. "The Maker's tests are never easy."

"Do you honestly believe we'll live through it?"

She returned to her preening. "What has that to do with anything? I said I would help. I have an obligation to fulfill."

"Which is fortunate for *him*," I said, nodding in the direction Kyp had flown off in, "and maybe all *he* needs to hear, but *I* need hope. I'm a thief, and a thief never does anything unless there is a chance of success."

She cocked her head at me. "Know this then, Thief. If ever any Crow had the Maker's blessing, it's Kyp. He led us out of the humans' hunt and through the storm. He snatched us out of the talons of the Collection. Kyp has more lives than Great Crow. If anyone can lead us underground through rats and darkness and up into that heart of the human roost — and find a way out again — it's him."

Chapter 38

Next morning, the sun rose, and for the first time since we'd arrived at the humans' colony, Kyf didn't send out any of the band. Instead we all foraged, found food, ate together and rested through to the latter sixth. Then Kyf gathered everyone together in an elm overlooking the lake, and Kyp spoke to them.

"There's no reason for us to wait any longer," he announced. "We think we should now be able to steal into the human's roost and release Kym. That's what we came here for, so that's what we'll do. I just wanted to tell you what I'm sure everyone here already knows: that we couldn't have done any of this without you. Your patience, your persistence and your spirit made this possible. Kwaku, Katakata, Erkala and I will go in together. I can't say when we will return, because once we are in the human roost, no one knows for certain what route we will take to escape. If things work out, we should return soon."

His gaze swept through the trees at the perching Crows. "There has never been anything formal among us — there is no bond of blood or word that keeps us together — but I am grateful to have flown and foraged together with each one of you. If we don't return, there are no obligations, you are all open to the wind. If anyone needs something more formal, let things go this way. Check with those penned inside the human roost. If they haven't heard from us within a day or two, something will have gone wrong. If you haven't heard from us within six days — don't wait any longer. Go wherever you can find food and roosts to suit you.

"I'd advise you to stay together regardless of what happens because, in the time we've flown together, I've come to see us as Family. And a Family continues regardless of which individuals come or go. So, stay safe and watch out for one another. The wind under your wings, Cousins, and good eating at the other end."

Kyf suddenly spoke. "Whatever anyone else thinks, *I* know you are coming out. I know because Kwaku wouldn't go unless he knew. The Maker will watch over you while you are inside, and we will wait here, on the outside, as long as it takes. Whatever else happens in there, there's good eating and a safe roost with us when you come out again, and … and …" Her voice trailed off. "Imagine that," she muttered, "I don't know what else to say."

Kyp glanced fondly at her, then looked up and around throughout the tree and bid the band a final "Good eating." In something approaching a single voice, they murmured "Good eating" in response.

I couldn't resist getting in my own last word, however. I halted at the very end of the highest branch as the others prepared to fly. "I know *he* said you could go if you haven't heard from us in six days. But *I'm* telling you, don't leave. Don't leave, because as surely as we're going in, we're coming out again."

That said, we flew down to the shore to meet the rats.

Chapter 37

I had told Erkala that I needed to pick up a few things I had cached away and would meet them at the waterside. They were waiting in a bush when I dropped to the rocks along the shore.

"So, what took you so long?" Kyp demanded. "And what are all those things you're carrying?"

"This is the thing we'll need to open the weaves," I said and dropped the thing on the ground. "Humans use their paws, but we should have better luck with one of these." Erkala picked it up.

"How did you get this?" she asked. "You never said."

"I plucked it from a human's ear."

Kyp, Kwaku and Erkala all made sounds of astonishment, which I secretly found very gratifying. "I just flew in close," I said, demonstrating the maneuver, "and pulled it out."

"Kata," Kyp chortled, shaking his head admiringly. "*That* was the work of a master."

Erkala put it down. "How will you carry it?"

"With a little shove, it fits nicely around my leg." I demonstrated and placed it above my right talon. "I'll just walk in with it there."

"And those?" Erkala asked, pointing. "What are they?"

"This *you* need," I said to Kyp, "to put around your neck." I lifted the glittering circlet and slid it over his head and neck. He turned his head this way and then that, trying to view it.

"Why?" he asked, slowly spinning.

"You can't tell right now," I said, adjusting it so it sat evenly on him, "but in the darkness part of it glows."

"Glows?" Kyp demanded, "How?"

"Some kind of human magic — they've pulled down a plume of the Sun Eagle. Who knows? You'll see, though. The twelve small dots along the edge of that round thing? They glow like tiny stars."

"Really?" Kwaku asked and brought his right eye in close to inspect it.

"Yes. In the darkness I should think we'll need whatever light we can carry. And this other one," I said, holding it up, "is a gift for our rat friends."

"Ah, very smart." Erkala nodded approvingly. "They like the shiny things."

"When did you get these?" Kyp asked as he stalked along the shore, still trying to gain some view of the glitter hanging around his neck.

"I've been gathering them ever since we started this nonsense about going into the human's roost."

Kyp shook his head admiringly again and felt the thing jiggle back and forth. "Kata," he said, "Crows will be sharing stories about you and telling them to their chicks in their roosts long after you have flown on. And *humans* will be telling stories to their little ones, warning them of the monster Crow who made off with everything that wasn't fastened down."

"Maybe so," I agreed, "but the story *I'm* most interested in hearing is the one that tells how we went into the human's roost and came out again safely. Does anyone know how that ends?"

"Let's find out," Kyp said. With that, we flew to the tunnel entrance.

At first glance the shore seemed completely deserted. Then I noticed, a little way into the tunnel's mouth, in the shadows, a pair of eyes watching us.

Erkala stepped forward and called. Kyrt and around twenty of the yearlings slipped away from surrounding trees, landed and dropped scavenge in a pile upon the rocks. They then turned and flew away. Kyrt called a quiet "Good eating" to us as he left.

We had only to wait a moment before the rat that had been watching us scrambled out. It was entirely black and as big as a very heavy cat — but nimble for all that. It approached the pile, sniffed it thoroughly and reared up on its hind legs. Then it cocked its head and squinted at us. I picked up one of the glitters, stepped forward and placed it next to the pile. The rat studied me carefully and scampered around to investigate the glitter. It sniffed at it, tasted it, took it in its teeth and shook it a little, then rose to his hind legs again and chittered. Dropping back to all fours, it pranced around the glitter several times more, sniffing it again for good measure, and finally slipped it over its head.

Erkala leaned in to me. "Shiny things," she whispered softly, "*very* smart."

Abruptly, the rat gave a sharp cry and from the surrounding rocks dozens of rats swarmed the beach. In an instant every bit of the scavenge disappeared.

To our great astonishment, Erkala then chittered something. The big rat bobbed its sleek head and turned, and we followed him to the tunnel mouth.

It was my turn to lean in close to Erkala. "Do you really think," I asked, "that he knows we want to go in there?" I nodded up at the human's roost.

"I certainly hope so," she answered quietly, "or we'll be attacked before we get fifty steps into the tunnel."

Chapter 40

This part of our journey is difficult for me to share. Difficult because it is the thing of which I am least proud. Difficult because it was created in my worst nightmares.

We climbed through the tunnel's dank mouth down into the black darkness, and for a time I feared I would never see light again.

It was thoroughly dark, dark in a way I had never encountered, in a way that is hard to even comprehend. Close your eyes: the blackness that perches there, behind your eyelids, is brighter than the darkness we met.

The sound of rushing water filled the tunnels. Pretty soon we became aware of other sounds.

Rustlings and scurryings — rats running alongside us, behind, in front. Everywhere.

As our eyes gradually adjusted to the dim-beyond-dim, the tiniest, almost imperceptible illumination was provided by the two glitters I had stolen from the humans. One at Crow height — Kyp. And the other sliding along, skittering, slipping sideways and rearing up. The rat leader. That faint green radiance gave me some small hope and kept me going. By that tiny luminescence, we began to detect dim shapes and movements. At first the tunnel's sides were glistening with dripping water and ooze, but soon a shifting, swaying, rustling, furry mat crowded about us as the rats completely filled the tunnel.

Under our talons the surface was at first slick and difficult to navigate. Then, all at once we encountered rubble and crumble, loose dirt and broken stone. The rat leader veered off the main tunnel and turned up to our right into a smaller, tighter channel.

Here, my feelings of dread so overwhelmed me I was almost unable to move. I fought to catch my breath, but the confinement, the sense of the tunnel pressing in around me, was so great it was as if the air was forced from my lungs. I inhaled a kind of compressed darkness instead. If there had been any way of going back other than that fetid tunnel teeming with rats, I would have turned and run. My fears grew until they filled that space so completely there was no room left for me. I feared that we would be overcome by the rats, that I would lose my way, that I would become wedged among the filth and debris, unable to move, and would be left behind and forgotten.

It was only Kyp's encouragement and Erkala's and Kwaku's insistent, relentless nudging that kept me moving.

As we climbed, the tunnel shrank. Parts crumbled under our talons. Slick, resilient cords or vines of some kind twisted and coiled about the tunnel's walls. We stepped over and around them and sometimes tripped on them.

Ahead of us, the two faint lights kept moving.

The tunnel narrowed still further and we were forced to proceed in single file. The rat leader suddenly reared and chittered and we stopped.

Erkala listened and chattered something back.

"What is it?" Kyp asked.

"I'm not sure," she answered slowly. "I think he's warning us. Something about this part of the tunnel. Something we have to be careful not to do."

As we continued climbing, we could smell something new — the sharp, eye-watering odor of burned fur and flesh.

The smell grew stronger. The rat chittered again. Erkala told us that we were to stay well to the right. A dim, flickering orange and red light appeared, and we began to detect a very soft buzzing sound.

"Don't touch the rats," Erkala called. "I can't make out what this one's saying, but it's something about 'touching them is death.'"

Then we saw them: three dead rats, frozen in positions of agony, part of their flesh burned — entangled among the smooth vines. Some of the cords were torn, or chewed upon, and it was from these that the flickering light snapped and spat. The buzzing and humming was strongest here. We crept past carefully, but whether it was because something disturbed them or because they were beginning to decompose, the closest rat toppled, showering the tunnel with a burst of brilliant sparks.

A little farther, the rats that had followed us dropped back; soon only a few were accompanying their leader. Then the leader turned and faced us, chattered something and disappeared.

"It said," Erkala translated, "that we are to go this way." We entered a new kind of tunnel, not one that had been dug or chewed out by rats, but a wider, smoother, more open passageway. Not big enough for humans to move through, but obviously made by humans. It was maybe two Crows high, three Crows wide. Big enough for a Crow to move about in easily. We had only just entered it when we heard an enormous whooshing sound and were enveloped by warm air pulsing through the tunnels strongly enough to blow our feathers back.

What did it mean? Was something coming? Kyp thought not. "I think this human roost is so big," he explained, "it has its own wind currents."

Erkala hesitated — without the rat leader, she was at a loss about how to proceed. Kwaku, who had been very quiet up until this time, suddenly spoke. "I've dreamed this place," he said in that quiet, thoughtful voice of his. "I know the way from here." It's a measure of how much we had come to trust Kwaku that without any further discussion, he led and we followed.

Kwaku moved swiftly, Kyp close by his side, the glitter around his neck giving Erkala and I something to follow. Sometimes we walked through the twisting tunnels. Other times, our path veered straight up and we flew. Finally, Kwaku stopped at a place where the floor was made of thin, crisscrossing slots. A dim red light radiated up through these openings. "Here," Kwaku said. "We have to go through here."

I peered down, directly beneath my talons. An open space much bigger than the tunnel was partially visible through the narrow punctures. Kwaku tapped at the corners of this slotted thing and tugged at a tiny stone, shaped like a tapered seed, embedded in the smooth surface. This, he told us, is what held the slotted thing in place. It made no sense to me, but I took a turn pulling at the stone.

Abruptly it came loose in my beak and clattered by my talons. Now, Kwaku told us to jump on the slotted thing.

We all took turns, pulling, stamping, jumping. The thing bent a little, and our jumps grew more energetic. Finally Kyp took an enormous leap and the corner where the small stone had been collapsed — and Kyp fell straight through.

That surprised and frightened us until we heard Kyp's voice from below calling, "Come on!"

Suddenly we heard a clamor of unfamiliar Crow voices shouting on the other side, scared, startled, excited beyond measure. Kwaku and Erkala dropped through the hole, and I followed. And — there we were. Inside that immense human roost, among all those captured Crows.

chapter 41

After the darkness of the tunnels, this roost seemed nearly bright, receiving starlight through the invisible stone barriers and some kind of red light from a glowing rock that was fixed to the wall.

From behind his weave, one Crow called to Kyp in a heavily accented voice, “You? You are for to help us?”

Kyp shushed him, saying, “Stay quiet or the human may come.”

We glided quietly over top of the weaves until we found the one we were looking for.

“Kyp,” a voice called from within the weave. “Good eating and a safe roost.”

Kyp folded his wings and dropped. He perched

next to the weave, cocked his head and peered closely through the stone columns. “Good eating, Kym, Good eating — and it’s been a long time coming.” The two briefly touched foreheads through the weave, then Kyp said, “Kata, let’s try that human ear thing.”

I flew over and removed it from my leg. Holding it carefully in my beak, I lowered it into the slot in the weave. I felt the curved end slip into place — and pulled! On the other side, Kym grasped the columns of her weave just above the slot and yanked upward. The weave gave a slight shudder and then — nothing.

“Try again,” I said.

We did, with the same result.

“What’s wrong?” Kyp asked anxiously.

“I’m not sure,” I replied, peering down the slot.

“It *should* just slide open,” Kym said, tugging on the weave. “Am I doing anything wrong?”

“Not that I can see. Let me try something,” I said and flew to another weave.

“What are you doing?” Erkala called.

“I’m going to see if this works on any of the others,” I answered and told the Crow inside — Koryn — what he had to do. I slipped the curved end into its slot and pulled. Koryn, watching for my signal, yanked up on the weave — and this time, a piece of the weave slid up and an opening appeared. Koryn hesitated, as though he couldn't believe what had just happened. Then he leaped out and flew tight circles around the roost, for the sheer joy of being able to use his wings. A thunderous roar rose up throughout the roost — cheering, shouting, congratulating Koryn, voices calling "Me next!" "No, me!" "Come open this one!"

I cautioned them to remain quiet and returned to Kym's weave. "One more time," I urged, and we repeated the whole routine. Again, nothing.

I asked if the human had ever had any trouble opening it.

Kym thought a moment. "Maybe. The last time, the human seemed to ... I don't know ... pull a little harder to get it to open. And jiggle it."

"Jiggle it?" I repeated.

She thought again, as though seeing it in front of her. "From side to side."

I nodded and looked more closely at the columns.

"This thing," I told Kyp, holding up the glitter I'd snatched from the human ear, "is doing what it's supposed to, but the ... the weave on this one is bent and it can't open. You see." Kyp peered where I had pointed. "The, twig, that holds this thing shut is pushed away — and so it *should* open. But the ... the flap thing can't slide open because it's catching on this corner, here, where it overlaps. You see?"

Kyp had been trying to follow, but still wasn't making sense of it. "So," he asked, "you're saying this … thing of yours won't open her weave?"

"No," Kym answered, understanding. "He's saying it *has* opened it. See? There." She pointed with the tip of her beak. "But the flap can't slide up because it's twisted. Is that right?" she asked me.

"Exactly," I said, nodding again.

We perched there and thought. At last Kyp turned to me and said, "I'll take care of this. You go let everyone else out."

"Everyone?" I asked, startled. "The jays and magpies —"

"No one gets left behind in this badger's warren. We'll take everyone out when we go." Kyp turned to Erkala. "Can you help him organize this? And where's Kwaku?"

"He's ahead of us, as usual. He's already among the other weaves," she answered, "telling the Crows to be patient, that we'll free them shortly."

Chapter 42

As Erkala, Kwaku and I moved through the roost opening weaves, Kyp crouched near Kym. "Maybe we could shift it," Kym suggested, "if you push from your side, to free the jam, and I push up from my side."

Kym leaned against the base of the weave and pushed, but her talons just skittered out from under her on that smooth surface. She hooked her talons to the weave's framework and pushed up. Kyp shoved from his side. The weave shuddered, slid a bit, then stuck again.

Kyp leaped onto the frame, grasping it in his talons and flailing his wings. "Maybe I can shake it loose." But the weave didn't budge.

"We've moved it a bit," Kym allowed.

"Yes." Kyp nodded, trying to catch his breath. "How much longer until the humans arrive?"

Kym glanced out through the invisible barrier. "It's starting to grow light outside," she answered. "We have a little while yet, but only a little."

Kyp grasped a column of the weave in his beak and rattled it.

"I'm grateful that you made such an effort to find me," Kym said quietly as she strained to pull the weave up. "What a surprise, what a huge surprise — what a gift it was to see you. And for you to make your way in here. It goes beyond thanking you. But you'll have to be getting yourself and the others out soon."

Kyp didn't reply, but instead wedged his beak under the gap they had created. "You pull," he grunted. "I'll push." Kym grasped the frame once more. The two exerted themselves, and for a moment it seemed nothing would happen. Then the weave gave a sharp whinge of protest, the flap lurched up a little farther — and shuddered to a halt.

In the space they had managed to wrestle from the flap, it was almost possible to slide one's head through. But above the gap, the weave had bent and twisted so badly that it now appeared completely stuck. No matter how hard Kyp and Kym shook, shoved and threw themselves at the flap, nothing could produce the extra few feathers of space they required.

"You'll have to go soon," Kym repeated. "You have an obligation to take these others out. If you can, come back for me."

Kyp squeezed his head as far as he could into the gap. "No," he said, bracing his legs under his body. "I'm going to push from down here. All we need is a slightly wider opening. Go!"

Suddenly the air around us was torn apart by a shrill, prolonged scream, the loudest I've ever heard. It seemed to come from above us, under us and inside us all at once, a scream — louder than a thousand Crows' — of pain and panic. What, I wondered as we all looked for the source, could possibly shriek that loud?

Then I realized it was the roost itself screaming. When I saw smoke seeping into the roost, I knew it was screaming "Fire!"

chapter 43

Smoke first crept through the cracks and edges of the roost and then began to billow in. I landed next to Kyp, who was still struggling to open Kym's weave. "Most of the others have been freed. There are maybe only six more to do."

"What are you doing here then?" he asked. "Get them out."

"I'm not needed. Erkala will have the rest of the weaves open shortly. How can I help here?"

"I've given up trying to slide the flap up," Kyp grunted. "I'm trying to bend this weave enough for Kym to crawl under."

I crouched beside him and stuck my head through, and we both pushed. Kym seized the weave with her beak and pulled. Nothing happened. We pushed again.

Kwaku landed, leaned in and quietly said, "One of the jays we freed flew around a corner and down some human tunnel. He said he saw flames."

Kyp pulled himself out of the opening and peered through the smoke. Several Crows had panicked and were throwing themselves against the invisible stones that covered the openings. "Stop them!" Kyp told Kwaku. "They're only hurting themselves. Gather them together and get them ready to leave." Kwaku flew to organize them.

Kyp turned to me. "As soon as Erkala has freed the others, I want you three to lead them out. Take this glitter" — he slipped it from his neck — "so that they'll be able to follow you through the tunnels."

"I don't know the way," I protested.

"Between Erkala and Kwaku and yourself, you'll figure it out."

I shook my head. "I'm not leaving without you —"

"I'll *follow*," he snapped. "This won't take much longer."

"But —"

"There's no time to discuss it. Get them all together. Lead them out." He looked at me. "I'll join you as soon as I can."

Erkala dropped beside us, coughing. "Everyone's been freed, but the tunnel we entered through is entirely blocked by fire."

Kwaku returned. "I have everyone together," he reported. "They're just waiting for you."

"But how will we get out now?" I asked.

"I don't know yet," Kyp answered, as a great stream of black smoke poured in. Behind it, flames were licking at the walls. "This shrieking will certainly bring humans. When they come in, there may be an opportunity for us to fly out. Keep everyone together, as far from the flames as you can."

Kyp turned back to Kym, crouched down once more. "Let's try again." He braced himself and pushed.

It's impossible to describe exactly what happened next, because several things happened at once. The roost seemed to shudder. There was a soft popping sound, followed by an angry roar and the sound of things collapsing. Then, with an immense blast of hot air, orange and red flames shot up and raced through the chamber.

In less time than it takes to blink, we had been entirely encircled by flames.

Chapter 44

"Kym!" Kyp called over the roar of the flames, "can you pull from the inside again? You three, can you perch up top and pull from there?"

Everyone positioned themselves. "Ready," Kym said as she waited for the signal to pull.

"Now!" Kyp urged.

We all heaved together. The weave groaned. The Maker must have been watching over us because she sent one of her miracles at that point. From above, water suddenly showered us, as though the rolling smoke was cloud, and rain was springing from it. The water quenched some of the flames and cooled us. Erkala raised her head to catch a drop in her opened beak.

"Again," Kyp called.

We heaved.

"Again!" Kyp grunted.

We strained again, all of us. The rain slowed to a trickle and then stopped. The flap seemed to slip a little. The edge of the weave cut deep into Kyp's shoulders. Suddenly there was a snap, part of the weave crumpled and folded up on itself, then the flap slid up. Kym stepped out.

Had we wanted to celebrate we would not have had the time, because at that moment the floor shivered and tilted. Human things clattered toward us, and we all leaped into the air, panicked. With a grinding, rasping groan, the roof to our right collapsed and a part of the floor fell away. Kwaku, hovering just behind me, shouted "This way, this way, this way!" and the Crows, magpies, jays and ravens followed him up through a splintered, gaping hole.

Chapter 45

The smoke was so blinding and the heat so intense it was hard to think. Everything seemed to be happening all at once, the roost crying in a great voice as it collapsed and crumbled. The fire roaring as it consumed everything. Hot, acrid air sweeping past. Things falling. Kyp shouting "Stay close, everyone stay close!" Kwaku calling "This way! This way! This way!" and my noticing that he had managed to snatch up the glitter so at times it was as though faint starlight shone from his back and penetrated the gloom.

We flew up until finally there was no "up" left. No exit, no opening, nowhere to fly, except back down into the darkness. But orange and red flames were licking up like the waggling tongue of an enormous black mouth waiting to swallow us.

"This way," Kwaku called.

"*This* way?" Kyp demanded. "What way?"

We followed the sound of Kwaku's voice until we were all huddled together in a tight corner near the very top of the roost. For some reason, a tiny bubble of something like clean air had accumulated, surrounded by smoke so thick and hot it choked and scorched at the same time. There, in that small space, fifty-some birds hovered and coughed.

"Where to now?" one of the Crows shouted.

"Wait" is all Kwaku would say.

"*Wait*? Wait for what?" the stranger demanded. "Wait to be burned? I say we have a better chance going back down."

"Kwaku has told us to wait," Erkala said calmly. "And there is nothing down there but fire."

"Wait," Kwaku repeated. "Just wait."

Abruptly, the Crow turned and flew back down. Kym called out to stop him, but either he couldn't hear or had already made up his mind. He disappeared for only a moment, then flared as flames devoured him.

"Maker of the Maker," I said to no one in particular, "it's hot in here."

"Be patient. Wait," Kwaku said.

Then Kyp turned and stared at Kwaku with a strange intensity. "You've already seen this, haven't you?"

Kwaku coughed. "Something like it."

"What happens?" Kyp asked. "Do we get out?"

Kwaku peered at him with a curious expression and, after a moment's hesitation, nodded. "There's release for everyone," he said, "if you just wait." Then, as if he had received a message, he called, "Wait for the breath."

Then we all felt it — like the entire roost drawing in a gigantic blistering breath, and the stone and wood and all the human makings trembled, and the air from down in the deepest part of the roost came swelling up in a great, searing blast of hot air, ash and smoke — and the roost began to come apart, blown out ahead of us.

"Now *fly*!" Kwaku shouted. As the roost expelled its breath and the walls collapsed, we were expelled as well, tossed into the tumbling chaos, past falling stone, past fire, past birds exploding into flame, the air so hot my eyeballs felt singed through my closed eyelids.

Suddenly, we were beyond the fire, beyond the smoke, able to breathe! I spread my wings. "We're out!" I cried through my cracked, parched throat. "We're out!" I looked at Kyp and saw his horrified expression. Then I saw him, too — Kwaku, falling from us, already a distance away, like a bright blossom on a black tree, spinning, engulfed in flame from wing tip to wing tip.

Kyp folded his wings and plunged after him.

chapter 46

We fell more than landed upon our roost's outstretched limbs.

The yearlings flew up to greet us, but their welcome fell silent in their throats when they came close enough to truly see us. There were, of course, many more bodies returning than they had been expecting. And singed, half covered with ash and exhausted, we must have seemed more like frightening specters than friends settling in the roost.

I felt the branch bend and turned in time to see Kyf folding her wings beside me. I saw her search every limb on the tree for Kwaku, then she looked to me. She said nothing, and tired as I was, I couldn't think of anything to say or any way to explain. We stared at each other until she simply flew from the perch to collect Kaf. Together they quietly settled in another tree, on their own.

"Good eating," I heard finally and turned to see Kyrt. The expression he wore was both joyful and curiously tense. "Good eating," I replied tiredly, wondering what could be making him anxious now that we had returned. Then I noticed, just behind him, two new, rather ragged-looking Crows. "Who are they?"

"Scouts," he answered. "Sent to find us by the Collection." He nodded at five of the larger Crows surrounding the two, guarding them. "Kyf noticed them, and she and Kaf and a couple of the others forced them down before they could go back and deliver our location."

Kyp, who had been perched beside me, breathing slowly and resting, opened one eye and croaked, "Don't let them leave." Then his head slumped to one side and he tumbled to the ground.

Chapter 47

I dreamed of Kwaku.

We were all perched in an immense tree. It was warm — more like late summer than winter. I say "we were all" there, but it was just a feeling, really. I heard voices, but never actually saw anyone but Kwaku.

He looked exactly the same as he always had. Very composed, very thin, feathers all askew. Those big calm eyes peering at me, like he knew what I was going to say before I knew what I was going to say.

He seemed to be readying himself to fly, and that upset me. I asked him where he was going and he answered that it was time for him to leave. I'm not sure what I said, but I know I protested and he told me not to worry, that we would all meet once again at the next Gathering. Then he told me to give Kyp a message. "Tell him now is good," he said.

"Now is good?" I asked, as confused as ever by his vague pronouncements. "What is *that* supposed to mean?"

"Just tell him," he said, nodding calmly. "He'll know."

He cocked his head and got that look he got whenever he heard someone from somewhere telling him something that none of us ever heard. So I asked him, "Is something coming?" He was busy listening, so I asked again. "Kwaku, is something coming?"

He turned and flattened one of those feathers that was always standing up — but for the first time ever that I could recall, that feather stayed down. He looked very pleased with himself. He said, "Don't you know? Something is *always* coming."

Then he was flying away. He hadn't leaped off the branch, so I don't know how he did it, but he was high in the air and had already traveled a great distance. He was farther than the moon and quite a ways past the stars, so I suppose it must have become night suddenly. But, curiously, as far away as he was, as small a dot in the sky, I could still hear him clearly. "Keep an eye on him."

"Who?" I shouted back.

"Kyp. He'll need your help. Even," he added, his voice trailing away into the distance, "when you think he's beyond help."

With that he was gone, and it was dark and quiet in that big tree. Without his even-tempered, slow-talking presence to irritate me, and teach me, and keep me company, I felt terribly alone.

That was the dream, yesterday night.

Cousins, one dream is ending and a new one beginning. Before the first can truly finish, though, a count must be completed.

Of the fifty-seven we freed from confinement in the human roost, forty-three are still with us. Two jays, three magpies and a raven were among those who escaped, and all but one magpie have since thanked us and flown on to find their own folk. We know six Crows perished in the flames: Kaleb, Kylwyt, Kur, Kymur, Kakawyt and, of course, Kwaku. Three others haven't been heard from and we assume they were consumed by fire or crushed under falling debris: Kutu, Kyr and Kwyk. Join me in silence as we honor their flight. They have finished their dreaming and have flown with the Maker to a place we have only dreamed of.

This is a time for honesty, and I will tell you the truth. For a time I feared Kyp would join them. After he fell, his breathing became shallow. Kym, Erkala and I urged him to wakefulness and he managed to rouse himself briefly and half fly, half walk to a quiet, protected spot in a thick grove of bushes. There he collapsed into a deep sleep, waking only fitfully. We set Crows to keep watch. Three days he slept, unable to eat or speak, fire blasted as he was from the inside, his throat and beak so scorched raw that he was barely able to swallow. Kym watched over him most, brought him beakfuls of water, fed him tiny bits of the softest scavenge.

Two days ago, for the first time since he followed Kwaku into the flames, he managed to say a few quiet words. It may be several moons before his voice will be heard from treetop to treetop. He felt it important that a message be relayed to you now, and I am only serving as his beak, telling you what he would tell you if he were well.

He asks me to tell you that he is grateful to all of you whose thoughts have been with him as you waited for him to recover. I told him of my dream and he said he understood at least part of it. He says Kwaku was right once more — "Now *would* be good." The time has come for us to leave the humans' colony.

So the ending to one story is also the beginning for another. We followed Kyp here, and we could stay. But what peace or safety can we expect, roosting within such close reach of humans? Winter is nearly done. It's the way of things that we should move. The only question is where and how.

Kyp proposes that we accompany him west, many days' journey to his previous Gathering grounds, where he is the rightful Chooser. There we would find good eating, a safe roost and — if there are any of his Clan who survived the Plague — additional Family to enlarge our numbers. It's a long flight and a hard flight, and we're certain to encounter risks along the way. But the risks can be no greater than the risks we would face if we stayed.

We have waited to call Forum only to see if Kyp could fly. He and Erkala have just now, just this sixth, returned from scouting, and he seems to have found his wings. Though his voice has not yet returned, and there are feathers that won't be healed until his next molt, he feels his wings will bear him the distance.

He believes there is some urgency for us to move quickly. As you all know, the Collection is strong, and though we caught their scouts and have kept close guard of them, no doubt others will be sent.

Some of you may feel doubt about our abilities to make this journey. After all, who are we? Outcasts, leftovers, a ragged band perched in a wilderness surrounded by humans. But more than anything else — Kyp reminded me when we spoke — we are survivors. Survivors, my Cousins. We have been tested by the Maker, and we have, all of us, passed. Passed through fire. Passed through water. Passed through barriers and darkness, disease and confinement, and the Maker has a gift for those who pass such tests. That gift is Family. That gift is a flock and faithfulness and trust. That gift is *us*, Cousins — us, and what we have given to one another, and what we have come to mean to one another.

I said it is a time for truth. Personally, I never expected to follow a Chooser again. I never expected to be part of a flock again, or fly in company with others, or feel what I feel for all of you. It comes as the greatest surprise to me to have companions that I care about and who care about me. It is an immense surprise — but a happy one. Cousins! Brothers and Sisters! Forage now, drink, rest and dream easy through the day. We have everything we need. We have Family to protect us, wisdom to guide us and a helpful wind to lift and carry us. We'll leave late in the last sixth for new Gathering grounds, new nesting territory and a new future.

May the Maker bless the route we take and guide us all to a safe roost at the other end.

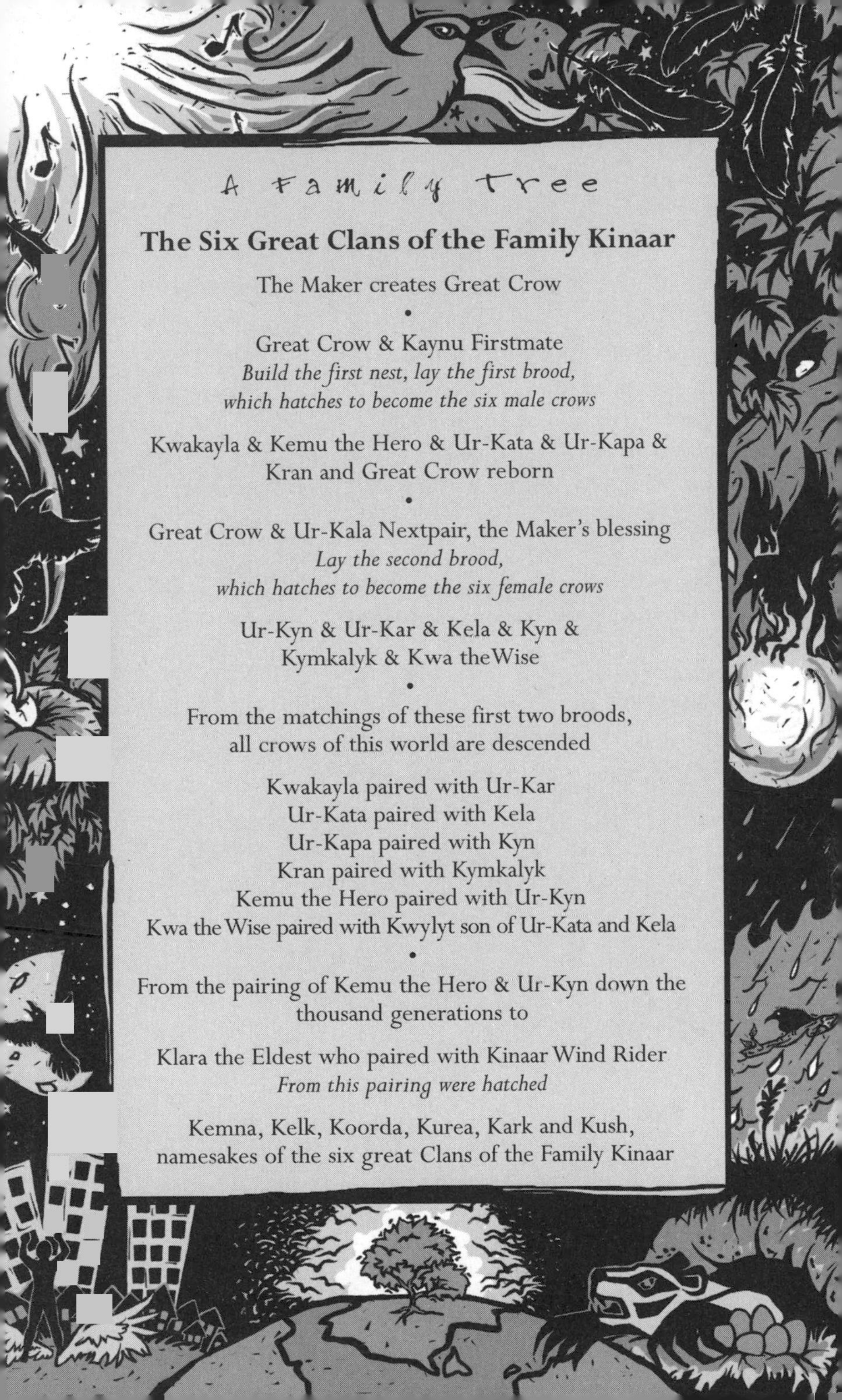

A Family Tree

The Six Great Clans of the Family Kinaar

The Maker creates Great Crow

•

Great Crow & Kaynu Firstmate
Build the first nest, lay the first brood,
which hatches to become the six male crows

Kwakayla & Kemu the Hero & Ur-Kata & Ur-Kapa &
Kran and Great Crow reborn

•

Great Crow & Ur-Kala Nextpair, the Maker's blessing
Lay the second brood,
which hatches to become the six female crows

Ur-Kyn & Ur-Kar & Kela & Kyn &
Kymkalyk & Kwa the Wise

•

From the matchings of these first two broods,
all crows of this world are descended

Kwakayla paired with Ur-Kar
Ur-Kata paired with Kela
Ur-Kapa paired with Kyn
Kran paired with Kymkalyk
Kemu the Hero paired with Ur-Kyn
Kwa the Wise paired with Kwylyt son of Ur-Kata and Kela

•

From the pairing of Kemu the Hero & Ur-Kyn down the
thousand generations to

Klara the Eldest who paired with Kinaar Wind Rider
From this pairing were hatched

Kemna, Kelk, Koorda, Kurea, Kark and Kush,
namesakes of the six great Clans of the Family Kinaar

Coming fall 2006

The Judgment

Book three, Feather and Bone: The Crow Chronicles

In this thrilling finale to the Crow Chronicles, Chooser Kyp faces the greatest test of his leadership. As the plague-ravaged crows flee south, pursued by the vengeful Kuper and his Collection, Kyp learns that deep divisions exist within his new flock.

Then, after a long journey, they must confront the Collection — and an even more fearsome force of nature.

Clem Martini
Ages 12 and up
1-55337-756-7 hardcover with jacket

Don't miss ...

The Mob

Book one, Feather and Bone: The Crow Chronicles

One of the most talked-about children's novels of 2004 is the first book in the saga of a family of crows who face troubled times. Murder and revenge mar the flock's annual Gathering, and the Chooser must decide on fit punishment. Then, an unexpected spring blizzard forces the crows to seek shelter in forbidden worlds ...

"Convincing, wholly absorbing."
— *Booklist*

"... a humorous and unique view of humans ... The writing is excellent."
— *School Library Journal*

"A shoo-in for the most original YA novel of 2004."
— *Washington Post Book World*

Clem Martini
Ages 12 and up
1-55337-574-2 hardcover with jacket
1-55337-664-1 paperback